24 HOUR LOTTERY TICKET

GAYLE TILLER

24 Hour Lottery Ticket

Copyright © 2010 by Gayle Tiller

ISBN-10: 1448675014
ISBN-13: 978-1448675012

This is a work of fiction. Names, characters, businesses, organizations, places, and incidents either are the product of the author's imagination or are used fictitiously. Any resemblance to actual persons, living or dead, events, or locales is entirely coincidental.

All rights reserved. No part of this book may be reproduced, scanned, or distributed in any printed or electronic form without permission, except in the case of brief quotations embodied in critical articles and reviews. For information, please e-mail gayletiller@yahoo.com or mail Gayle Tiller PO Box 720068 San Jose, CA 95172.

First paperback printing: February 2010.

Printed in the United States of America.

10 9 8 7 6 5 4 3 2 1

Gayle Tiller

This book is dedicated my former writers' group partners Mariann Jackson and Julie Newman.

Acknowledgements

I would like to give a big thank you to my former writers' group partners Mariann Jackson and Julie Newman. You are my inspiration and I appreciate all the great advice you gave me during our meetings.

I would like to thank my brother Bryce Tiller for his comprehensive input on the book. I also would like to thank my friends who took the time to read the entire book. I appreciate all of your great suggestions. Finally, I would like to thank those who read portions of the book. I appreciate your comments.

Chapter One

April 19, 2009 1:37 p.m.

I stared at the stack of bills in front of me. After being in law practice as a sole practitioner for three years, I still had a hard time. There were times when I wanted to shut down my office, but I couldn't. I had no place to go.

The county refused to promote me after I had passed the bar. My boss wanted me to stay at my old job as a housing specialist. She said I didn't have what it took to be a good lawyer.

I then applied at numerous law firms in Silicon Valley and not one single firm was interested in me. Maybe it was because it had taken me five times to pass the bar and I had graduated with a C average from a fourth tier law school.

24 Hour Lottery Ticket

Taking hypothetical tests and getting good grades never had been my thing. I was better at real life projects. And for some reason, law firms were more interested in academics than my twelve years of housing experience with the county.

I wanted to practice law so I had no choice but to start my own business. I left my $60,000 a year job and opened an office in downtown San Jose.

I thought clients would come in droves because of the location. It took almost three months before I got my first client. After that, clients trickled in, but not enough to make any real money. I tried everything to increase business: a web site, ads, joining nonprofit boards, and a referral panel but nothing worked.

After three years, my savings and 401k were gone. I was living off credit cards and they were almost maxed to the limit.

I heard a knock at my office door. I glanced at my calendar and it showed that I did not have any appointments. I didn't want to answer the door. It could be bill collectors and I had nothing to give them.

I ignored the knock and went back to looking at my bills. The knock became louder. I walked to my door, peered out my peephole and saw an older woman.

"I know you're in there," she said as she banged on the door. "Open the door now."

Jesus Christ, these bill collectors were getting bolder. Why couldn't they leave me alone?

"Ma'am, it's Sunday. We're not open," I responded.

"Dammit, I need to see you," she snapped.

"I don't have anything to give you."

"Stop playing games," she hissed. "Open the door now."

"No."

"It's an emergency and I need you to help me on my case."

Did she say case? Oh God, I hope I hadn't pissed her off. I opened the door for her and told her to come inside.

The woman walked into my lobby. She was about 5'2" with a slender figure. Her reddish brown hair was styled in a short cut with wispy bangs that accented her dark brown eyes and diamond shaped face.

The woman's white cotton pants and lavender short-sleeved polyester-blend blouse complemented her olive skin. Her face looked like she was in her early fifties, but I could tell from her hands and neck she was somewhere in her sixties.

The woman's face fell as she took in a quick view of my small, narrow lobby. There were a couple of chairs with discolored grayish-white cushions and an old cheap brown metal table that had a few of last year's magazines on top of it.

She glanced at the peeling brownish-green wallpaper and stained beige carpet. When she made a wry face, I wanted to apologize.

When I had started practicing, my first law office was a lot different. I rented a beautiful loft with large glass windows and hardwood floors. My furniture had been state-of-the-art. Two years later, I moved and sold my furniture, because I wasn't making enough money to pay the high rent.

I found my current office through a friend. The landlord agreed to rent to me for free in exchange for managing the six office spaces in the building. I was on the bottom floor with two other units and three were above me.

I made a gesture to the woman to sit down. She refused. The woman walked toward me. She then looked me up and down to take in the full length of my 5'10" height.

"You're Dianne Canton the lawyer, right?" the woman asked.

"Yes," I replied.

"I wasn't sure because you look a lot heavier than your picture."

Picture? She must mean the picture on my web site. It was over three years old. It was taken when I was in decent shape. But after my break-up with Shawn, I stopped exercising. Luckily, my scale was broken. So I had no idea what I weighed. I was sure that it was a lot, because rocky road ice cream was the only thing that gave me pleasure these days.

"I guess I need to get a new picture," I mumbled.

The woman made a sour face when she gazed at my stomach. Her look made me wish that I hadn't worn light-colored jeans, which emphasized my thick thighs and belly and a red t-shirt that tugged against my ample breasts.

She stared at my thick, curly dark hair that fell just below my shoulders. The woman almost formed a smile, but she couldn't for some reason. She then looked down at the stained carpet and grimaced. She looked back up at my face and focused on my emerald green eyes.

"I can't believe you thought I was homeless," she huffed.

"No, I didn't," I replied.

"Then why wouldn't you open the door?" she asked.

"Because I don't do business on Sundays," I lied.

"You need to make an exception for me," she demanded.

"Maybe," I countered.

"You will," she snarled as she pulled out an old newspaper.

"Were you in a story?" I asked.

"No, I wasn't. Just read the numbers."

I peered at the newspaper. "These are winning lottery numbers from a long time ago. What does this have to do with anything?"

She pulled out an envelope from her purse and removed a faded ticket. She then held it with both hands.

"Look at the numbers," she said as she showed me the ticket.

I peered at them and smiled. "It looks like you're the winner."

"Tell me something I don't know," she sneered.

I glanced at the newspaper again. "But this newspaper is six months old. Have you filed a claim?" I asked.

"No. It's due tomorrow."

My eyes widened. "Tomorrow!" I exclaimed.

"I have 180 days to turn in the ticket and tomorrow is the deadline."

"But why have you waited so long?"

"Because I didn't want the publicity," she replied.

"And now you want to file a claim?" I asked.

"I don't know," she responded as she put the lottery ticket back into the envelope.

"Why are you afraid of publicity?" I asked.

She inhaled and her hands trembled. She tried to speak, but her lips would not move.

"Ma'am, are you wanted for a crime?" I asked.

"No, it's nothing like that," she replied.

"Then I don't understand why you won't file," I said. "The lottery ticket must be worth millions."

"73 million," she responded.

"Tell me why you would walk away from 73 million dollars."

"Because the media destroyed me once and I won't allow them to destroy me again," she responded.

"How did the media hurt you?" I asked.

She wiped tears from her face. "They took away everything I had worked for."

"What is your name?" I asked.

"It's not important," she answered.

"I can't help you if you don't give me your name," I said in an irate tone.

"Did you grow up in San Jose?" she asked.

"No, I didn't," I replied. "I came here in the late 80s."

"When in the 80s?" she asked.

"1989, after I graduated from college."

"Then you wouldn't know anything."

"About what?" I asked.

"What happened back in 1986," she replied.

"No one would care about something that old."

"You don't understand," she snapped. "The media never forgets."

I wiped my brow. "Ma'am, did you kill someone?" I asked.

"Absolutely not. I've never committed a crime in my life."

"Have you ever been charged with or indicted for any crime?" I asked.

"No," she responded.

"If you don't have a criminal history, I don't understand why you have a problem with turning in your lottery ticket."

"I told you why," she murmured. "It's the media."

"You won't tell me what happened and you won't tell me your name," I said as I folded my arms. "I can't help you without this information."

"My name is Emma Watkins," she said while glaring at me.

"That name sounds a little familiar, but I can't place it."

"I told you that you wouldn't know who I am."

"Mrs. Watkins, you have until tomorrow to turn in the lottery ticket," I said. "What exactly do you want me to do?"

"I'm divorced so it's Ms. Watkins," she responded. "And please call me Emma."

"Okay, Emma. But you still didn't answer my question."

"I need you to research whether I can legally avoid publicity. If I can, I will file the claim along with a restraining order that will prevent my name from being released to the media."

"Why would you need a restraining order? Is there any domestic violence involved in your case?" I asked.

"No, there's not." Emma frowned. "Restraining orders aren't just for domestic violence cases. They're used in other cases in which the court orders another party not to do something. In my case, the court would order that the lottery is restrained from releasing my name."

"Now, I understand what you want," I said.

"Good." Emma smiled.

I took a deep breath and said, "Emma, I need more information before I can commit to taking your case. Tell me what happened."

Emma stared into my eyes. She exhaled deeply. "Give me an hour and I will tell you everything."

Chapter Two

Emma's face dropped when she walked into my 400 square foot office. She was disappointed by the fact that it did not look any better than my lobby. My couch was a futon with a black cover and two grayish-black pillows. Next to it was a tiny refrigerator and microwave.

There were three non-descript black metal folding chairs propped against one of the walls. My six-foot long oak desk was chipped in several places with a large crack on its left side. My second-hand office desk black leather chair had a split down its middle.

The air conditioner buzzed in the background. Emma winced when she heard the noise. She folded her arms and turned to view my law degree.

"I've never heard of your law school," she remarked.

"It was founded back in the late 80s in east San

Jose. It was a night school for working adults. It went out of business about two years ago."

"How many times did it take you to pass the bar?" she asked.

"Five," I responded. "Most of my classmates never passed."

Emma rolled her eyes and muttered something under her breath.

"What did you say?" I asked.

"Nothing," she answered.

I handed Emma a chair and motioned her to sit down. She took the chair and sat down in it next to my desk.

I sat down behind my desk and pulled out a yellow pad and pen. I cracked a smile and said, "Emma, can you tell me who referred you to me?"

"My neighbor Cindy Wooten recommended you," Emma replied.

Cindy had been a client in a landlord-tenant case. She lived in low-income senior housing and she had found love in her late sixties. Cindy and her partner Donald were inseparable. On a regular basis, Donald spent the night at Cindy's apartment. The manager of the complex was a busybody who had nothing better to do than watch who entered in and out of tenants' apartments. The manager accused Donald of living with Cindy and served Cindy with an eviction notice.

We were able to show that Donald lived elsewhere. The manager later withdrew the eviction notice. Because Cindy only lived on social security, she was unable to pay my normal fee. Instead, she paid me with weekly home cooked meals.

"Cindy was a great client," I said. "So can you tell me what happened twenty-three years ago?"

"I was a Superior Court judge in Santa Clara County. I presided over a case that involved a defendant who was accused of selling drugs out of his apartment. The defendant's landlord let the police in to search his apartment. The police found drugs and firearms.

"Because the police had failed to obtain a search warrant, the defendant's rights had been clearly violated. As a result, I had no option but to dismiss the case."

"That seems reasonable," I said.

"Right. A few weeks later, the defendant went on a shooting rampage. One person was killed."

"I'm sorry that happened."

"For my opponents, it was the perfect case to launch a recall campaign against me. The victim had all American looks. She was nineteen, attractive and blond. Her killer was African-American, who had a long criminal history. The race card had been cast and they ran with it."

"The race card?" I asked.

"You haven't heard of that being used as a tactic?" Emma asked.

"Yes, I know what it is," I answered. "I was just trying to find out more information."

"Good," she said while folding her arms. "You aren't prejudiced against African-Americans, are you?"

"No," I said.

"Are you sure?"

"Absolutely," I responded. "I know that most people can't tell what I am. But I'm mixed with African-American. My father was African-American."

"I thought you were Italian or maybe Latina," she said as she stared at me in disbelief.

"I'm mistaken all the time for different ethnicities," I replied. I wasn't in the mood to discuss my experience as a racially ambiguous person. I needed a case and not a session of therapy.

"Like your father, my husband was African-American," she said while looking at me directly in the eyes. "They used that against me. Back then, interracial couples were not accepted.

"During the recall campaign, they flashed a picture of my husband and me alongside the killer of the girl in their TV ads. It was a subliminal message that I had been easy on the defendant, because he was African-American.

"The San Jose Black Coalition called the ads racist. Mainstream groups dismissed the ads as good campaigning."

Emma paused for a few seconds and wiped a tear from her left eye. "Then there was the campaign slogan."

"The campaign slogan?"

"Bad court decisions kill innocent people. That slogan played over and over on TV and radio."

Emma pulled out a faded newspaper from her bag and handed it to me. The headline read, "Voters Oust Judge Watkins."

I stared at the headline for a few seconds. "Emma, I'm sorry what happened."

"After I lost the recall election, I would drink myself into oblivion and crawl into bed," Emma said. "The bottle was the only thing that I had in my life. Everything else did not matter."

"What about your husband?"

"A week before the election, my husband left me."

"I can't believe he left you when you needed him."

Emma paused for a second and looked down at her hands. Her upper lip quivered slightly. "It was their fault."

"Whose fault?"

"The media."

"How?"

The phone rang as Emma opened her mouth. I looked at the caller ID. It was Shawn.

"You can take the call," Emma said.

"That's okay. It's not important." I let the phone ring until it went into voice mail. I wasn't interested in talking to Shawn. I had left him months ago. There was nothing he could say or do to make me go back.

"I need to go to the bathroom."

I told her that the bathroom was down the hall. Emma then got up from her chair and walked toward it.

I reflected on what Emma had told me. I felt sorry for her, but there was no way the court would grant a restraining order. Yes, the campaign had been ugly, but most campaigns were.

Right now, it looked like she did not have anything. I already had spent thirty minutes with her. I hoped I wasn't wasting my time.

Chapter Three

Emma returned from the bathroom. She sat down and folded her arms.

"Emma, tell me how the media destroyed your marriage," I said.

Emma unfolded her arms. "My ex-husband Michael was a brilliant man who cared about the community," she said. "In our marriage, there were times when he could be distant. He could be unsupportive. I felt so alone in our marriage."

"I don't understand what the media had to do with the break-up of your marriage," I said.

"Dianne, you need to be patient and let me finish my story," Emma snapped. "In my court, I had a law clerk. Brad was young and bright. The minute I saw him I felt a surge of electricity. It was like I was somehow connected to him."

Emma paused for a few seconds and fiddled with her ring finger. "I knew what I was feeling was not right. At the time, he was in his mid-twenties and I was in my early forties. He was way too young for me. And I was a married woman. For the next year and half, I kept our relationship strictly professional. But my feelings for him would not go away."

"So what happened?" I asked.

"Like you, Brad had trouble passing the bar. His girlfriend had left him and he had no friends. He told me about his fears and I told him about my unhappy marriage. I don't remember who made the first move, but we made love a week or two later in my chambers. There was no turning back. He made me feel alive. Brad had awakened my passion for life."

As Emma spoke, my mind drifted to Shawn. When I first moved into my office, Shawn and I had made passionate love on my desk, rug and futon.

I drifted back to the present. I then turned to Emma. "We all make mistakes," I said.

"My affair was not a mistake. It was something I needed."

"Okay."

"They somehow found about my affair."

"They?" I asked.

"My enemies who wanted to oust me from office," Emma answered.

"Oh."

24 Hour Lottery Ticket

"A week before the recall election, they printed excerpts from a letter I had written to him."

"What did the letter say?" I asked.

"In the letter, I wrote how much I cared for him and how our lovemaking made me feel alive and wanted. He was keeping me together during the recall election and he was my reason for living."

"Where did the excerpts run?" I asked.

"They sent a campaign piece to Santa Clara County voters a week before the election. That evening, when it hit TV and radio, I knew that my life was over."

I did not know what to say to Emma. So instead, I looked into her eyes for a few seconds in silence.

Emma cleared her throat. "My husband packed his things, took our daughter, and moved into his mother's house. I tried calling him to apologize, but he would not answer my calls."

"You have a daughter?"

"Yes. Jenny was 15 at the time. She's 38 now. Jenny has never forgiven me."

"I'm sorry. Things could change in the future," I said. Her daughter seemed to be very immature. Although I was only three years older, I knew I would have supported Emma in her time of crisis. I had always done that with my own mother.

"I doubt it," Emma replied.

"What happened to your law clerk?" I asked.

"He resigned after the story came out."

"Did you continue to see him?" I asked.

"No," Emma answered. "After the story broke, he stopped taking my calls. I went to his apartment and he would not answer his door."

I was at a loss on what to say to Emma. So I said nothing.

Emma stared at the floor and then looked up at me. "They took everything away from me: my husband, my daughter, and my lover." Tears welled up in her eyes. "They destroyed my life."

"Emma, I'm sorry about what happened," I said in an earnest tone. "Do you know how they obtained your love letter?"

"That I don't know. I had enemies everywhere."

"Do you think your lover could have given them the letter?"

"No, that was not in his nature," Emma answered.

I was stunned by Emma's unyielding trust in her law clerk. It was almost as if she had been blinded by the affair.

Emma shook her fists. "I cannot and will not go through again what happened twenty-three years ago."

"Emma, you told me that after the recall, you went on a drinking binge, correct?" I asked.

"Yes," Emma replied.

"So at some point, I am assuming you stopped."

"It took over six months to wean myself from the bottle. There have been times over the years when the bottle has beckoned me back. Sometimes I give into it and sometimes I don't."

"So your drinking has been an issue on and off over the years."

"Yes, it has," Emma responded.

"I am sorry to hear that," I said.

"Don't be sorry. We all have demons that we fight against."

I thought about my own demons and decided it would be best not to talk about them. Instead I said, "Emma, so at some point, you went back to work."

"About eight months after the election, I found a job."

"As a lawyer?" I asked.

"No, I knew that I could never be a part of the legal profession again. I found something that had nothing to do with the law."

"What was it?"

"I was an office manager for a small research studies nonprofit. I was totally out of the limelight and the work suited me just fine. I worked there until I retired a couple of years ago."

"But in the beginning, your co-workers must have known about the election."

"The executive director did, but my past did not matter to him. He was very liberal and quite understanding. Back then, I was the only paid staff and it was not until a few years later our staff increased."

"Since the recall have you suffered any adverse consequences?"

Emma's eyes narrowed. "I told you about the loss of my family."

"No, I am talking about how you were treated by others after the results came in."

"A few months after the election, I received an anonymous letter saying the real reason for the recall."

"What was it?" I asked.

"They said the election had been a ruse to launder drug money," Emma answered.

"How?"

"In a countywide election, there are no limits for campaign contributions. Drug money was given to the recall campaign through phony contributors and expenses were fabricated."

"How much money was laundered?"

"Over a million dollars."

"Did you go to the police?"

"The police? Absolutely not," Emma answered. "The letter said they were involved."

"Do you have the letter?"

"I did at some point, but I misplaced it."

"Anything else?"

Emma clasped her hands. "There were the hang up calls and death threats. After I received the letter, I would get hang up calls several times a day and sometimes they would threaten me. The last time I got one was a few months ago."

"Did you know where the calls came from?"

"Back then, we did not have caller ID. About ten years ago, I got caller ID but it never showed anything."

"What about star 69?"

"I tried that as well but it never worked."

"Did you ever change your phone number?"

"No, I did not. I kept that same number, because I hoped that my daughter Jenny would call me but she never did."

"You have not spoken to your daughter since the election."

"We have seen each other a few times in person and the conversation has been always strained. She still blames me for everything."

"I'm sorry," I said.

"Two years ago, Jenny got married. She did not invite me to the wedding. Instead, her step-mother came in my place."

"I guess Jenny never learned the importance of forgiving."

"No, she has not. Are you close to your mother?" Emma asked.

"My mother's deceased," I replied.

"Was it cancer?"

"Yes," I lied. I did not want to tell Emma the truth. When I was 17, my mother died at the age of 39 in a car accident in which she killed three other people from a bout of drinking. That night, I had begged her to give me her keys but she wouldn't.

"I'm sorry. What about your father?"

"He's dead too," I replied. My mind drifted to when I first had come to San Jose in 1989 to find him. All I had was a picture and a newspaper clipping that he had been a professor at San Jose State. The trip had been a waste of time. My father had died a couple years before my trip. My father's family members refused to meet with me in person. Despite this, I liked San Jose. So I stayed.

"I'm sorry about your parents."

"They died a long time ago," I said while looking at the wall. "Emma, the easiest way to resolve your case is to find someone who can act as a surrogate and claim the ticket in his or her name. You could pay a fee and that way your name won't be in the media."

Emma's eyes narrowed and her face reddened. "Are you crazy? I would never hand over my ticket to a stranger."

"How about a relative?" I asked.

"Everyone in my family with the exception of my daughter is dead."

"Maybe you could ask your daughter for help."

"I am not going to bribe my daughter with money," Emma replied.

"What about a friend?" I asked.

"I have no one who I trust," Emma responded. "You are my only hope."

"Maybe I could claim the proceeds for you and give them back to you," I said.

"You must be out of your mind," Emma snapped. "I would never give you my ticket."

"You misunderstood me. I meant I would file the claim as your attorney and I would not provide your name. After I received the proceeds as your representative, I would release them to you," I said.

"The rules of the lottery don't give you this option," Emma responded. "The only way we can prevent publicity is through a restraining order."

I stared at Emma for a few seconds. "I will take your case on a contingency fee basis with a retainer of $1,000. This means that if we successfully restrain the lottery from releasing your name, my law office will be entitled to 1 percent of the proceeds."

"That's over $700,000. That's ludicrous for a few hours of work," Emma snapped. "I will pay $1,000 and not one dollar more."

"Then go somewhere else," I responded.

"No, you will be my lawyer," Emma snapped.

"Emma, this conversation is over," I said.

"No, it's not," Emma said. "Dianne, I really need your help. I will pay the $1,000 retainer fee. If you win my case, I will pay you an additional $50,000."

"I'll take your case for $500,000 contingency fee," I countered.

"$75,000," Emma responded.

"$250,000," I countered.

"100,000," Emma said.

"Let's split the difference for $150,000," I said.

"$125,000," Emma countered.

"Deal," I said.

"Good." Emma smiled. "I can pay you $500 now for the retainer and the rest in May."

"The deadline for the lottery ticket is tomorrow. I need the money now."

"I don't get my social security check until May. I really need your help."

"Emma, I will accept the $500 as partial payment." Five hundred dollars was better than nothing and it would help pay a bill or two. So I had no choice but to take it.

"What's next?" Emma asked.

"I'll need to type up our agreement," I said.

I drafted the agreement and handed it to Emma. She read the document slowly and signed it. Emma then opened her purse, took out her wallet and handed me five one hundred dollar bills.

"I really appreciate you taking my case," Emma said.

"You're welcome. I need to do some research. If you want to go home and wait for me to call you with my findings, you can do that. Or you can wait in the lobby."

"I will wait."

"Good." I then walked Emma to the lobby.

Chapter Four

I picked up the phone and called my best friend Robyn. I had known Robyn since my days with the county. Robyn had worked for the county for about eight years as its public information officer. She hated her supervisor, because he was a micromanager. She quit after she found a job with a small public relations firm.

"Robyn, I need to ask you a question."

"What is it?" she asked.

"You've worked on a lot of grassroots campaigns, right?"

"I would not say a lot. Maybe a handful."

"I would consider you an expert."

"I haven't won any of them."

"Why not?" I asked.

"To win a campaign, you need money," Robyn replied. "I've never been good at raising money."

"Why do you need money?"

"Dianne, when you're running a campaign, you are marketing a message. You need money for publicity like campaign literature, TV and radio ads. The more publicity people see, the more likely that they will vote for your candidate."

"So it's all about the money."

"Right."

"Do you know how much it would cost to run a countywide campaign?" I asked.

"Four or five million."

"What about a campaign twenty years ago?"

"I don't know."

"Can you give me an estimate?"

"Probably half of that."

"Who would finance the campaign?" I asked.

"Companies, wealthy folks and traditional grassroots fundraising."

"What percentage would be companies?" I asked.

"It depends on the issue. Grassroots would be a small percentage like ten to twenty percent. The rest would be companies and wealthy people."

"Aren't there contribution limits?" I asked.

"Not for a county campaign," Robyn responded.

"So a company could give as much as they wanted," I said.

"Yes, they could," Robyn answered. "Why are you digging up a twenty year old campaign?"

"It's confidential," I said. "How can I get copies of the campaign reports?"

"The campaign is too old to be online. The Registrar of Voters might have the reports," Robyn answered.

"Do you know anyone who works there?" I asked.

"I know a couple of people. You can call my cousin Jack tomorrow morning," Robyn responded.

"I need to see the reports now," I said.

"Dianne, it's Sunday," Robyn countered. "They're closed. You can't get anything until tomorrow."

"Tomorrow will be too late," I said.

"Why?" Robyn asked.

"I can't really discuss it," I said. "You know attorney-client privilege."

"Are you still coming over to my parents' house for dinner?" Robyn asked.

"Yes," I replied. I really liked Robyn's parents. When I first met them years ago, they readily accepted my bi-cultural heritage of being the daughter of a Jewish mother and an African-American father. Because I wasn't raised with religion, Robyn's parents taught me about Judaism.

The phone was silent for a few seconds. "Dianne, are you staying away from Shawn?" Robyn asked.

"I've been on the straight and narrow for over eight months," I answered.

"Good, because married men don't leave their wives."

"Robyn, I don't need a lecture."

"Stay away from Shawn. He's no good."

"I need to go." I didn't have time to talk to her about Shawn. I had a case and that took priority.

"I'll talk to you later."

I hung up the phone. I turned on my computer and clicked on my Internet browser. I performed a search for the disclosure rules for the lottery.

I read them and found that everything Emma had said was true. I looked up lottery cases in California and found there was nothing on point. I later found a case in Louisiana that was very helpful. The court ruled that the name of the lottery winner who was a former public figure could restrain the release of his name if he could show that he would suffer irreparable harm.

However, a mere declaration was not enough to shield him from publicity. There was a two-part test: 1) What were the past news stories about him? and 2) Why would publicity now cause irreparable harm?

I typed in Emma's name in a search engine. Nothing came up. With the recall of a judge, there should have been something. However, because it occurred such a long time ago, maybe it was too old.

I then went to the archives of the newspaper. The archives only went back fifteen years. The only other way that I could obtain copies of the media coverage was through the library.

I looked at my watch. It was only 2:47 p.m. The library closed at 6:00 on Sunday. So I had time. It would take about five minutes to walk to the library.

I turned off my computer, put my cell phone in my purse and locked the door. I walked to the lobby. I invited Emma to go to the library with me. She declined. Emma made it clear that she wanted to wait.

"Emma, do you have a cell phone?" I asked.

"I did, but I lost it a while ago," she answered.

"I'll give you my cordless phone in case you need to reach me," I said. "Just wait here while I get it."

I then walked back to my office and unlocked the door. I went inside and retrieved my cordless phone. I then locked the door and walked back to the lobby. I handed Emma my cordless phone and gave her my cell phone number.

I told Emma not to worry about answering my phone. Emma nodded her head as we said our goodbyes.

Chapter Five

I entered the media archives section of the library. Within a few minutes, I found several stories about Emma.

Murder of San Jose State Cheerleader Could Have Been Prevented

By William Stokely, Staff Writer

April 24, 1986

Longtime community leader Wilcox Rushton stated at a press conference yesterday that the murder of San Jose State nineteen-year-old cheerleader Valerie Lotson could have been prevented if Judge Emma Watkins had not dismissed a previous case against the alleged murderer Rickey Sellers.

"An innocent girl died two days ago, because of Judge Watkins' senseless decision," said Wilcox Rushton. "Because of a legal technicality, Judge

Watkins dismissed a case against Sellers. Two weeks later, Sellers' guns were returned. One of the guns was used to kill the victim."

On March 25, Sellers appeared in Judge Emma Watkins' courtroom. He had been charged with selling cocaine.

In the case, there were several statements from witnesses that Sellers was a known drug dealer. His apartment later was searched and a pound of cocaine was found along with several guns registered in his name.

Sellers' attorney John Finister argued that the search was illegal on the basis that the police failed to obtain a search warrant. Deputy District Attorney Vanessa Whitehead argued that the search was legal because consent was given by Sellers' landlord.

On March 26, Judge Watkins ruled in favor of Sellers' attorney. In her decision, she wrote the following: "Although a landlord is the legal owner of the property, the consent for a search of a tenant's apartment must be given by the tenant. Accordingly, because the defendant was a tenant of the said property, no consent was given. As a result, a proper search was not conducted."

The victim's family had no comment about Judge Watkins' decision.

Funeral arrangements will be held on Saturday, April 26 at Rose's Chapel at 2 p.m.

Two weeks after the murder, Sellers was found dead in his jail cell with a suicide note confessing to the murder. Wilcox Rushton used the confession to bolster his claim against Emma.

It was no surprise he had later mounted a campaign to recall Emma. Rushton's blame clearly had been misplaced. Emma simply had done her job. The case was a clear violation of the fourth amendment. If Emma had not made her ruling, ultimately the Supreme Court would have found that the defendant's rights had been violated.

Was Rushton simply a misguided citizen or was there something more to him? That I could not tell from the articles.

I glanced at the next article with the headline, "Judge Watkins Caught Fooling Around with Her Law Clerk." My stomach began to ache. To make a mistake in private was one thing, but to have it blasted all over the news was another.

As I began to read the article, I felt a tap on my shoulder. I looked up and it was Shawn. To say he was handsome was an understatement. He was downright gorgeous.

At 39, Shawn still took care of himself. He was 6'2" with broad shoulders, a trim waist and muscular thighs. His bronze complexion complemented his hazel eyes and thick, jet-black silky curls. His Mexican mother had given him high cheekbones and an Aztec nose and his African-American father had given him full sensual lips.

"Can we talk outside for a minute?" he asked.

I stared at the floor. I had made a mistake in coming to the library. But I had no choice because of

Emma's case. And I hadn't expected Shawn to work on a Sunday. When we were seeing each other, he normally worked during the week as the assistant librarian.

"Dianne, all I want is a minute of your time," Shawn pleaded.

I nodded my head and walked with him into the hallway.

"Dianne, why aren't you returning my calls?" Shawn asked.

I stared at him and said nothing. He knew the answer.

"Dianne, I've been worried about you. I went to your apartment and there was an eviction notice."

"They must have posted it on the wrong door," I lied.

"Dianne, your neighbors told me you moved."

"Yeah, I did a few weeks ago."

"Where are you living now?" Shawn asked.

"Shawn, I need to get back to my research. I'm working on a case."

"Dianne, I need to see you."

"I'm busy."

"I really need to see you," he repeated. "Things haven't been going well since my wife Lauren lost the baby."

That baby had been the reason for our break-up. Lauren and Shawn had been separated for over six months. Shawn had been living in the den of their house. Lauren got drunk one night and begged Shawn to make love. Shawn felt sorry for her and gave her what she wanted. Her birth control failed and she got pregnant.

Shawn didn't want her to have the baby. But Lauren was against abortion and she didn't want to raise the baby alone as a single parent.

Shawn never had known his real parents. He had grown up in foster homes. He wanted to do the right thing with his own child. So Shawn felt he had no choice but to stay with her.

I looked Shawn in the eyes and said, "I'm sorry about your loss. Maybe you can try again."

"Dianne, I've moved out," he said. "It's over."

"I need to get back to my research," I said as I turned to walk back.

"We're getting a divorce," Shawn said.

I turned away. I wanted to believe him but I knew better. Shawn had told me that before and it turned out to be a lie.

"Dianne, my wife filed for a divorce. If you don't believe me, you can check online."

I stared at him and said nothing. Shawn followed me as I walked back into the media archives room. I logged onto a computer and went to the court's site. I typed in Shawn's name and found a case.

Three weeks ago, Lauren filed an action for dissolution of marriage. I smiled. Shawn had told me the truth.

"How about after you're done, we go to your office and talk?" Shawn asked.

"My client is waiting for me there," I replied.

"Then let's talk here," Shawn said while he gently touched my hand. "There's a conference room down the hall."

I wanted to say "no" but I couldn't. I had waited five years for him to be free. I didn't want to lose him now. So I had no choice but to go with him.

We entered the conference room. It had a large table and a couple chairs with four barren walls and no windows.

Once we were inside, Shawn shut and locked the door. We then sat down.

"Dianne, I've missed you so much," he said. "You are the only woman I want. I think about you 24 hours a day."

I felt a tingling throughout my body. The truth was I missed him as well. I had tried dating one or two men after him. But it wasn't the same. The sex had been lousy and we didn't connect on any other level. After eight months of being away from Shawn, I needed him.

I looked at Shawn as he walked toward me. He wrapped his arms around me and embraced me. Our tongues danced while we caressed each other's bodies.

"Dianne, I want to show you how much I love you."

"We can't do it here," I said while shaking my head.

"I'm the only one who has the key," he said. "Come on baby, I need you now."

"Shawn, I think we should go somewhere else," I stammered.

"We belong together right now and right here," he responded.

Every part of me wanted him. I looked into his eyes and kissed him hard. Shawn then began tugging off my clothes. And I did the same with him.

Shawn laid down on the floor and whispered, "I want you to love me."

"But I've gained weight," I protested.

"More curves to love," he said as he caressed my body.

"Really?" I asked.

"Baby, you're so beautiful," he said. "I love all of you. I love your gorgeous green eyes, your hair and luscious curves." Shawn then pulled me toward him.

After Shawn protected us with a condom, I got on top of him. Shawn caressed my body while I rocked back and forth. He said things to me that made me feel wanted, desirable and beautiful.

I rocked harder and harder until my body exploded four times. Within a minute after my last orgasm, Shawn reached his own climax.

Shawn stroked my face and said, "Baby, you are so good to me."

He held me for a few minutes. We put back on our clothes. Shawn kissed me lightly while he unlocked the door.

"I'd like to see you later tonight," he said.

"Shawn, I have a lot of work to do on this case," I responded.

"If you need anything, just call me." Shawn smiled.

I nodded my head and walked to the bathroom to refresh myself. I felt so alive and wanted. Shawn and I could now be open with our relationship. In due time, we would join our hands in marriage. With Shawn by my side, things would get better with the business. I felt like I could do anything.

I smiled when I glanced at my watch. I had only an hour left to finish my research.

Chapter Six

I walked back into the media archives room in the library. I found a few articles. I glanced at the first couple and there was nothing remarkable.

I read the third article and it stated Wilcox Rushton had died in 1987 from a heart attack. He had been a community leader and an instructor at a local community college. Mr. Rushton apparently had been a man of modest means.

Emma's conspiracy theory did not make sense. There was no way that Rushton could have been connected to a money laundering operation. Perhaps, Emma's overdrinking had made her a little paranoid.

But I felt something was missing. I did not know what it was. As I turned to leave the library, my cell phone rang. I flipped it open. It was Emma calling me.

"Hi Emma, I should be back in the office in a few minutes."

"Dianne, I need to step out for a bit. I'll be back by 6:30."

"Okay. I'll see you then," I said.

"Dianne, did you see your friend Shawn at the library?"

"Shawn?" I asked. I had told Emma specifically not to answer my phone. It could have been a bill collector. I didn't want Emma to know my financial business.

"I guess you didn't see him," she said. "He called a while ago. I told him that you were at the library."

"Were there any other calls?"

"Only his. By the way, if you need to call me, my home phone number is 555-2743."

"Thanks."

After we said our goodbyes, I hit the end key on my cell phone. I looked at my watch. The library would be closing in a few minutes.

A divorce would take about a year. That would give me plenty of time to lose the weight I had gained. I wanted to look good for my wedding day with Shawn. A civil ceremony would suffice or maybe something small and intimate.

I logged into my e-mail. I sent a brief e-mail to Shawn with my new cell phone number. I had changed it since we had broken up a few months ago.

24 Hour Lottery Ticket

    I logged off the computer and walked out of the library. God, I felt good. Finally, I would get everything I wanted. But there was still Emma's case. So far, I hadn't found anything. Unless I found something soon, going to court tomorrow would be a waste of time.

Chapter Seven

April 19, 2009 7:03 p.m.

Emma was thirty minutes late. I called her phone number. The phone rang several times until an answering machine came on. I left a message for Emma to call me.

The clock was ticking away and every minute made a difference. I wasn't going to wait all night for Emma.

I looked at Emma's address on my notepad. She lived in the same senior housing complex where my previous client Cindy lived. The complex was only a few blocks from my office.

I turned off my computer and gathered my belongings. I put a note on my door for Emma to wait for me in case she showed up.

Within a few minutes, I was at Emma's senior housing complex. I buzzed the lobby door and no one answered.

I tried again until a small hunched-back elderly woman answered the door. I told her who I was. She then opened the door.

I walked to the elevator and boarded it. I rode up to Emma's floor. I knocked on Emma's door. There was no answer. I waited a few seconds. I knocked harder. There still was no answer. I tried again for the third time. I waited and Emma did not come to the door.

As I was tacking a note on Emma's door, it slowly opened. Behind the door was Emma. Her eyes were bloodshot. Her breath smelled like cheap liquor.

"I knew you would come for me," Emma slurred.

I peered inside Emma's apartment. There were stacks and stacks of books and newspapers piled almost six feet high. The carpets were stained and there was a musky odor.

I felt like chastising her. Couldn't a grown woman take care of herself properly?

"Emma, what happened?" I asked calmly.

"Life," she answered.

"Life?"

"Yes."

One-word questions and one-word answers were not going to get us anywhere. Tomorrow was the deadline and something had to be done now.

"We need to get you some coffee," I said.

"I think I have some in here somewhere."

There was no way I was stepping into Emma's apartment. "Emma, I have coffee at my office," I said. "Let's go there."

"That's fine. Where's your car?"

"It's in the shop," I lied.

"Didn't they give you a loaner?" Emma asked.

"No," I replied.

"Why not?"

"Because they didn't. I don't mind walking. It's good exercise."

"We can drive my car. I don't think I should drive, because I've had a couple drinks."

"A couple?"

"More like five or six, but who's counting?" Emma giggled like a schoolgirl.

"Emma, where's your car?"

"In the garage," she said.

I told Emma to follow me. We stepped into the elevator. I pushed the button to the parking garage.

Emma leaned on me until we reached our destination. I then took her hand and helped her walk into the garage.

She pointed to an old 70s faded red Mustang with rust on its roof and doors. The left door had a dent and the front bender was slightly cockeyed. Years ago, it might have been a beauty. Now, it looked awful from years of neglect.

"Does it run?" I asked.

"Of course, it does," Emma slurred.

"Where are the keys?"

"In the car."

"Why?" I asked.

"So I won't lose them," Emma replied.

"Okay." That made sense. If she left them in her apartment, it might take days to find them.

I started the car and beckoned Emma to get in. Emma's body trembled as she sat herself in the passenger seat.

"Dianne, I don't feel good," Emma said as she grabbed her stomach.

"Emma, turn down the window," I yelled.

Like a child, Emma obeyed my order. She then stuck her head out the window and heaved. She stopped for a few seconds and then heaved again.

Emma wiped her face. She turned to me and said, "I feel better."

My stomach turned. I had to use all my willpower not to vomit.

Within a few minutes, we were at my office. Emma wobbled out of the car and threw up on the street.

"I just had to do it one more time. It won't happen again."

I hope she was right. We then walked into my office. I sat Emma down while I made her coffee.

"This is good coffee," she said.

"Thanks."

"You're good at taking care of me. You must be experienced."

I said nothing. There was no way that I would tell her about the countless times I had taken care of my mother when she had gone on her drinking binges. That was none of Emma's business.

"Thanks again for your help," Emma said.

"You're welcome," I responded. "I wanted to tell you what I found from my research."

"Can we stop them from publicizing my name?" Emma asked.

"Emma, everything that I found has been published in the papers: the death of the cheerleader, your affair and the recall. I don't think previously published material is grounds to prevent the lottery from releasing your name. We need something more."

Emma's eyes widened. "Like what?"

"We need to show the money laundering link. That has not been shown before. If your name is released, we could argue that they would come after you and you would be irreparably harmed."

"So let's do it."

"I need evidence. The only thing that I think that might help us is the Registrar of Voters' campaign reports. But unfortunately, the office is closed until tomorrow."

"So we can go tomorrow and get the reports."

"On Mondays, the court only has one restraining order calendar. We have to file our application by 8:30. The Registrar of Voters opens at 9:00. So it will be too late to get the campaign reports."

"There has to be another way to get the report."

"I tried a friend whose cousin works for the Registrar of Voters and she couldn't help me."

"Call her again," Emma demanded.

"What for? There's nothing she can do."

"Let me call her."

"That's not going to change anything."

"It might," Emma said.

"If you want to talk to my friend, that's fine."

I dialed Robyn's phone number and hit the speakerphone key. The phone rang a couple of times until Robyn picked up.

"Robyn, I have you on speakerphone. I have Judge Emma Watkins with me. She wants to talk to you," I said.

"Hello, Judge Watkins. How are you?" Robyn asked.

Emma tapped her foot and said, "Robyn, I am no longer a judge. So just call me Emma."

"Sure, Emma," said Robyn.

"Robyn, I don't know if you know anything about me. I was recalled from the bench years ago," said Emma.

"I was in high school with your daughter Jenny. So I remember the recall," said Robyn.

Emma looked as if someone had just slapped her. She took her face in her hand and began to massage the side of her face.

"You went to school with Jenny," Emma said.

"Emma, yes I did," Robyn replied.

"I guess you know the full story," Emma said slowly.

"It was ugly. Emma, you should not beat yourself up about it. The past is the past and you can't change it," Robyn said in a soothing voice.

Emma's face brightened a little. "Thank you for being so kind."

"So why are you calling me about something that happened long ago?" Robyn asked.

"Robyn, I need the recall's committee campaign reports," Emma answered.

"Why do you need reports that are over twenty years old?" Robyn asked.

"It's confidential," Emma replied. "I understand that your cousin works in the Registrar of Voters' office," Emma said.

"Yes, he does, but he won't be at work until tomorrow," replied Robyn.

"Robyn, I can't wait until tomorrow. We need the reports tonight," Emma pleaded.

"I don't know if I can get the reports tonight. I will see what I can do," Robyn said.

"What if I call your cousin?" Emma asked.

"No, you don't need to call him. I can do that," said Robyn.

"How about we all meet at the Registrar of Voters in an hour? Emma asked.

"I'll see what I can do. But don't blame me if we can't get in," Robyn replied tersely.

"We will get in. We will see you in an hour," Emma said.

"See you in an hour," Robyn replied.

Chapter Eight

Emma and I waited for Robyn outside of Emma's ancient car in the Registrar of Voters' parking lot.

I shivered from the cold night air. Robyn was already thirty minutes late. This was so unlike her. She was normally punctual when we met.

"When is your friend coming?" Emma asked in an irritated tone.

"Emma, I called her cell phone twice and she didn't answer," I said.

"Maybe her cell phone battery went out," Emma said.

"Maybe it did," I replied.

My cell phone rang. I picked it up and said, "Hello."

It was Robyn. "Dianne, I'm on the way," Robyn said. "Jack is with me."

"Good, I'll see you in a bit," I said. I then hit the end button.

"She'll be here in a few minutes," I said.

"I knew that she would come through for us," Emma said smugly.

We waited in silence. Robyn's car pulled up. Robyn got out of her car with her cousin Jack. Robyn was short and round with dishwater blonde curly hair and porcelain white skin. On her left hand, she proudly wore her wedding ring. Six months ago, Robyn had married her longtime boyfriend Mark.

Jack was somewhere between his late 30s and early 40s. He and Robyn looked like they could be brother and sister. His body was soft and round. At 5'10", Jack and I were about the same height. No one would call him handsome. He wasn't ugly either. He was just in the middle.

I said hello to Robyn. I then walked up to Jack and smiled. "You must be Jack. Thank you for coming."

"No problem. I'm always ready to help," he said.

Robyn's eyes narrowed a bit. She looked like she wanted to say something, but instead she was silent.

"Robyn and Jack, this is former Judge Emma Watkins," I said.

Emma shook their hands. "I'm glad that you both could come," Emma said while flashing a smile.

We then walked to the Registrar of Voters' office in silence. Jack used his passkey and the doors opened.

"The old reports are in the back in boxes. It might take a while before I find them. If you could wait in the lobby, that would be great," Jack said.

"That's fine," Emma replied.

Robyn tried to fake a smile. "Great. I really need to go to the restroom," she said. "I will be back in a few minutes."

"I should have done the same thing before I left my office. I'll go with you," I said.

"Sure," Robyn said.

Robyn and I walked briskly to the women's bathroom. We then entered the bathroom.

"You know Dianne, it wasn't easy to convince Jack to meet us here," Robyn said. "For this, he wants me to write a press release about his book. It's self-published and awful, but I didn't have the heart to tell him the truth."

"Thanks for the favor."

"No problem."

"So what do you think about Emma?" I asked.

"She's pushy and abrasive," Robyn said while brushing her hair. "But she knows what she wants and how to get it."

"Yes, she does."

"So Dianne, what's the real story? And don't give me that attorney-client privilege bullshit," Robyn said.

"Robyn, if Emma gives me permission to tell you, I will. But you know, I can't," I replied.

"Whatever she needs these reports for, it'd better be good."

"Believe me, it's important. That's all I can say."

Robyn and I returned to the lobby. An hour passed and Jack had not found anything. I was beginning to feel antsy. Perhaps, this visit to the Registrar of Voters had been a waste of time.

I turned to Emma and said, "I'm sorry this is taking longer than I anticipated."

"Things that take time are worth waiting for," she said calmly.

"Jack is good and he will find the file," Robyn interjected.

I wanted to say what if there's no file. Instead, I said nothing. There was no point in upsetting Emma.

Another fifteen minutes passed and Jack finally emerged with a file in his hand.

"I found the report," he exclaimed. "But there's something odd about it."

"What?" I asked.

"It lists all the contributions for the recall campaign," Jack answered. "However, for the major contributions and campaign expenses, the names are smeared with a white, opaque correction fluid."

"Why would someone put this substance on the pages?" I asked.

"It's illegal to put correction fluid on official reports," Jack responded. "However, it's possible that a county worker spilled it by accident. Perhaps, they did not report the incident because they were afraid of being disciplined. Or perhaps, it was done intentionally. There's no way to know."

"Is there any way to tell when this happened?" I asked.

Jack pulled out the report and showed us the pages. "It could have been done recently or it could have occurred a long time ago. I really have no way of telling."

Robyn turned to me and asked, "Dianne, why is this important?"

"Because if it happened a long time ago, maybe it was part of some concerted effort to cover up what happened," I responded. "If it happened recently, it's probably just an accident."

Emma cocked her head slightly and peered at the report. "Jack, couldn't a lab analysis tell how old the correction fluid is?"

"Ma'am, I suppose it could," Jack replied.

"We need to go to a lab," Emma said.

"Emma, it's after 10:00 on a Sunday," I protested. "We're not going to find anything open this late. Perhaps, that's something we can explore later."

Emma's face reddened and her mouth became twisted. She blasted, "Dianne, we don't have time to do it later. I need that analysis by tomorrow morning."

Jack turned to Emma and said, "Ma'am, without a court order, I cannot release the original report. So your lab analysis will need to wait."

"Can we scrape it off to see what's underneath?" Emma asked.

"That's not only a violation of a county rule. It's also a crime to deface an official document," Jack answered.

"That's stupid," Emma snapped. "How can it be a crime when the substance defaced the document?"

"Look lady, I don't care what you say. It's a crime. I'm not going to jail for some twenty year old recall campaign."

Emma glared at Jack and said nothing.

"Jack, does the report say who the treasurer was?" I asked.

"Wilcox Rushton," he replied.

"We should go talk to him," Emma said.

"We can't," I replied. "He died back in 1987."

"I bet they killed him," Emma said.

"The newspaper said he died from a heart attack," I said while I handed Emma a copy of the article that I found at the library.

Emma glanced at the article and shook her head. She muttered something under her breath. I ignored her. I turned to Jack and asked, "Can you make a copy of the report?"

Jack said, "Sure, no problem."

"Are you willing to sign a statement about the condition of the report?"

"Yes," he responded.

"Can I use your computer to draft the statement?"

"Dianne, I can't let you do that. It's county property and I could get into trouble."

"If I dictate the statement, can you draft it?" I asked.

"I can't do that either," Jack answered.

Emma stared at Jack in anger. "You must be with them," she snapped. "You don't want to help me."

"Look ma'am, I don't know who you're talking about, but I have to follow the county's rules."

"Jack, you've done a lot tonight," I said. "I really appreciate it. Would you be willing to come to my office tonight and sign a statement?"

"Tonight? It's getting late. I have to be at work in the morning."

"Jack, I want to thank you again for all you've done. We're going to court in the morning. So we need the statement tonight. I know it's a lot to ask for, but I hope you will consider signing it," I said.

"I'm sorry, but I can't do it," Jack replied.

"I understand you're busy with your new book and all."

Jack's eyes widened. "You know about my book."

"Yes, I do. Robyn told me about it and I'd really like to read it."

"Really? It's science fiction and set in the year 2250. Everyone is dead except for one couple who were on the verge of breaking-up prior to the war."

"I love science fiction," I lied while flashing my eyes and playing with my hair. "Tell me the title and I'll order it online. Or better yet, maybe you could drop off an autographed copy tonight at my office."

"Tonight? How about tomorrow?"

"Jack, I really want to start reading your book and I really need you to sign the statement."

"I can't do it tonight."

"Jack, I know you're busy, but my client's life is at stake."

"What's her case about?"

"I can't tell you that."

"Dianne, do you really want to read my book?"

"Absolutely," I said while licking my lips.

"I'll come to your office. After you read the book, can you write an online review?"

"Absolutely," I lied. There was no way I was going to review his book let alone read it.

"Great. I'll be at your office in twenty minutes."

"Good," I smiled as I handed him my business card.

I waved goodbye to Robyn. She looked at me with disbelief. She and Jack then got in her car and departed.

Emma turned to me and said, "You're good. You have a way with men and that's what we need."

I smiled and said nothing. I beckoned Emma to the car. We then got in and drove away.

Chapter Nine

April 19, 2009 10:34 p.m.

A few minutes later, Emma and I were back at my office. When I turned on the lobby's lights, a water bug scurried across the floor.

Emma made a wry expression. "You need to tell your landlord to spray for bugs."

"They just did. I guess that they didn't get all of them."

"I hope a bug doesn't jump into my purse and infest my apartment."

"Emma, you'll be fine."

"I hope so or I'll sue you."

I was tempted to tell Emma to "go to hell." Instead, I ignored her and walked into my office. I turned on my computer and drafted a statement for Jack to sign.

While the statement was printing, I heard a knock at my door. I walked to the door and let Jack and Robyn in.

I pulled out a couple of folding chairs for Jack and Robyn. They sat down.

Jack pulled out his book from his bag and handed it to me. "It's autographed. I hope you enjoy it."

"I really like science fiction," I said. "I'm sure it will be great."

"Really?"

"Yes," I lied again as I handed Jack the statement.

"Dianne, the statement looks fine," Jack said.

I handed him a pen and said, "Great, please sign here."

Jack signed the statement and handed it back to me.

"Jack, I will make you a copy."

I made a copy for Jack and handed it to him.

Robyn turned to me and said, "I need to use the restroom."

"It's down the hall."

"I need to go too," Emma chimed in.

Jack watched them as they walked out of the office. He then turned to me and said, "Dianne, do you need me for anything else?"

"No, I don't," I said while straightening the papers on my desk. "Thank you again for coming here."

"Okay," he said. "But before I go, I need to ask you something."

"What?"

"I don't meet a lot of girls who like science fiction and are good looking. Your green eyes are just out of this world. I was just wondering if we could go out some time."

"I'm seeing someone," I said.

"Is it serious?" Jack asked.

"Yes," I answered. After Shawn got divorced, he and I would be walking down the wedding aisle.

"He's a lucky guy," Jack said. "If you two ever break-up, give me a call."

There was no way that would ever happen. Shawn and I were soul mates. I said, "It's getting late and I need to get back to work."

"I understand."

Robyn and Emma then walked back into my office. Jack turned to Robyn and said, "I guess we need to get going."

"Thanks again for everything," I said as I waved goodbye.

"And don't forget about what I said." Jack smiled.

"I won't," I replied.

Jack and Robyn then left.

Emma sat down. "He likes you," she said.

"I don't know about that," I replied.

"He likes you," she reiterated. "But fat men are bad in bed. They have little..."

"Emma," I interrupted. "I have a lot of work to do."

"Okay," Emma said as she stretched out her arms. "But you're kind of chubby. They say fat women are more sensual. So maybe two fat people making love wouldn't be so bad."

Emma was truly getting on my nerves. I was tired of her insults, but I knew better than to argue with her. Instead, I got up from my chair and escorted her to the lobby.

"Please wait here until I'm done."

"Okay."

As I turned to go back into my office, I saw Emma slumped in the chair. Her eyes were shut and she was snoring quite loudly.

How could she have fallen asleep so quickly? It wasn't that late. Maybe the booze had gotten to her.

Perhaps, this was good. I could work on drafting the restraining order without Emma bothering me.

Chapter Ten

I pulled up the template for the restraining order and began drafting. Ninety minutes later, I was almost done. I just needed to ask Emma a couple of questions and we could call it a night.

I tapped Emma's shoulder. Emma would not wake up. I tapped her again and said in a low voice, "Emma, I need to ask you some questions."

Emma stirred slightly. "Let me go back to sleep. I have a headache."

"It's after midnight and I would like to finish the paperwork for the restraining order."

Emma opened her eyes and said, "Get me something for my headache. The light is hurting my eyes."

I opened my desk drawer where I kept a bottle of aspirin. I pulled out the bottle and it was empty. "I'm sorry, but I don't have anything for you."

Emma stared at me in disbelief. "Then go to the store and get me something now."

"There are no twenty-four hour stores in this neighborhood. The nearest one is a few miles away. Let's finish the paperwork, then you can go in a bit."

"Dammit, I want something now! My head feels like it's going to explode," Emma screeched.

"Give me your car keys then."

"You'll take good care of my car, right?"

"Sure."

Emma opened her purse and handed me the keys.

"I also need $5.00."

"Just advance me the cost and bill me later."

Advance her the cost? My checking account had nothing in it and I was already almost at the limit for my overdraft protection.

"Emma, this is not a cost related to the case. So I can't advance it."

"I will give you the $5.00 then."

Emma opened her purse and pulled out a bag of quarters. She counted out twenty quarters and gave them to me. "Here's the five dollars. Bring me back the change and a receipt."

I shoved the quarters in my purse and mumbled, "Thanks."

24 Hour Lottery Ticket

"When will you be back?"

"In thirty minutes."

"Good, I can go back to sleep." Emma said as she shut her eyes.

I left my office and headed toward Emma's car.

Twenty minutes later, I was heading back to the office with Emma's generic brand pain reliever. It only cost $3.09 with tax. Emma should be happy.

As I turned onto the block for my office, I saw blue lights flashing in my rear view mirror. I slowed Emma's car down and pulled over to the curb.

The police car parked behind me. A short, chunky thirty-something female police officer with a beer belly approached me.

"Ma'am, do you know that you did not signal when you made your right turn?"

"Officer, I did turn on my signal."

"No, you didn't."

"I did turn it on. I don't know why you didn't see the blinker."

"Ma'am, I'm going to have to cite you."

"Cite me?" Dammit, a citation would mean driving school and at least a hundred dollar fine.

"Ma'am, I need to see your driver's license, car registration and insurance."

I opened Emma's glove department and retrieved the registration and insurance card. I then opened my purse and took out my driver's license. I handed them to the cop.

"This car is ancient," she exclaimed. "It was made in 1973. It's two years older than me."

I looked at the cop and said nothing.

"Is this your mother's car?" the cop asked.

"No, it belongs to a client."

"A client? What kind of work do you do?"

"I'm a lawyer."

"A lawyer," she said as she rolled her eyes. "And where is your car?"

"It's repossessed."

"So you're driving a client's car."

"That's right."

"You know impersonating a lawyer is a crime."

I felt the heat rising in my face. "I'm a real lawyer. I may not make a lot of money, but I am doing the best I can."

"The next thing that you will tell me that there are doctors who are homeless."

"Officer, I don't know about that," I said as I pulled a card from my wallet. "Here's my bar card."

The officer peered at my bar card and handed it back to me.

"It looks real. So where's your client?"

"She's back at my office."

"It's almost 1:00 in the morning. Counselor, don't lie to me."

"Officer, with all due respect, my client is at my office. We have an emergency case. If you want to see her, my office is just one block up."

"Counselor, for some reason, I believe you."

"Are you still going to cite me?"

"Of course, I am. You didn't turn on your blinker."

"I did turn it on. Maybe the blinker isn't working." I then made a motion to turn on the right blinker. "Is it on?"

"No, it's not working."

"So I turned on the blinker in a car that I don't own and it wasn't working. That's not my fault."

"I won't cite you on the failure to turn on the blinker. But I'm citing your client for a defective blinker."

"Officer, my client is a poor elderly woman. Can't you give her a warning?"

"I don't do warnings."

"Officer, can't you make an exception? This is not my car. My client didn't know the blinker was not working. I can pass on the warning to her and tell her to get it fixed."

"Can you tell me why you're meeting your client so late at night?"

"Officer, I can't. It's attorney-client privilege."

"Counselor, I like your style. Nevertheless, I am issuing the citation for the turn signal. Tell your client to get it fixed."

"I will." Emma would not be happy.

The officer wrote the citation and handed it to me. She motioned me to sign it. I signed the citation.

She then gave me a copy of the citation along with my driver's license, Emma's car registration and insurance card.

The cop walked back to her car. I turned on the ignition and drove to the office while I cursed.

Chapter Eleven

April 20, 2009 1:03 a.m.

When I walked into my office, I could hear Emma snoring loudly. She was stretched out in her chair. I tapped her lightly on her shoulder. "Emma, wake up. I have aspirin for you."

"Jesus Christ, I was in the middle of a good dream. You should have waited," she snapped.

I wanted to tell Emma to shut up, but instead I said nothing. I handed her the aspirin, change and receipt.

"What is wrong with you? This is the store brand. I thought you were going to get me something decent."

"I wanted to save you money."

"I don't want this. You need to go back and exchange it," Emma wailed.

"Emma, it's after one in the morning. You have two options. Take the aspirin or take nothing."

Emma's face fell and she looked at me as if she were a small child. "I will take the damn aspirin. Where's your water?"

I pulled out a paper cup from my desk and handed it to her. "You can get water from the bathroom sink."

"Tap water? You're kidding, right?"

"No, I'm not. Take it or leave it."

Emma got up like an obedient child and went to the bathroom with the cup.

A few minutes later, Emma came back with a sour look on her face. She handed me back the cup. I took the cup and threw it in the trash.

I handed Emma the citation. "While I was driving your car, I received a ticket because your turn signal was not working."

She put on her glasses and looked at the citation. "The turn signal works. All you have to do is tap it a few times and it will start blinking."

"And how was I supposed to know that?"

"Anyone would know that."

"Whatever," I said.

"You're going to pay for the inspection of my car to show that it was working, right?"

"It wasn't my fault."

24 Hour Lottery Ticket

Emma's face turned into a snarl. "You can't do anything right. You are totally worthless."

I bit my tongue. I wanted so badly to yell at Emma and call her names. Instead, I said, "You may not like me and that is fine. But we need to finish the paperwork for your case tonight."

"I wish I never had come to you."

I ignored Emma's comment and handed her the pleadings for her case. "Here's what I have drafted. I need to add another statement about why you waited until the last minute to contest the publicity of the lottery ticket."

"It took me time to decide on what to do," Emma answered.

"179 days? That's a long time."

"Not all of us like to make snap decisions. I believe in mulling over my alternatives."

"Okay. Is there any other reason?"

"Also, I had misplaced the lottery ticket."

"So you lost the lottery ticket."

"I had the lottery ticket in my file of important papers. About three or four months ago, I could not find it. I looked through everything in my apartment and it was missing. So I figured it was gone."

Given the fact that Emma's apartment was a pigsty, her statement was not a surprise. "When did you find it?"

"I was going through my papers to look for the forms for my taxes. That's when I found the lottery ticket."

"When was this?"

"Two weeks ago."

"And you waited until just now?"

"I told you that I had to go over my options."

"And you waited until a Sunday to see a lawyer?"

"I did not pick a random lawyer. I've been studying you for awhile."

"What do you mean by that?"

"After I got a referral about you, I researched you on the Internet. There are over fifty online articles about you. It took me a while to read all of them. You really believe in doing what you do. I knew I could trust you and you wouldn't swindle me out of my lottery ticket. That's why I came to you."

"Thank you," I replied. The articles made me appear that I was a successful community lawyer. However, the reality was that the articles rarely generated any clients. I turned back to my computer, drafted the addition to Emma's declaration and printed it out.

I handed her the declaration. "Please review it and let me know if you want any changes."

Emma put on her glasses and read the document in silence. "This is great," she smiled.

"Any changes?"

"No."

"Good, please sign it then."

Emma signed the declaration and handed it to me. "Are we going to win?"

"We'll see."

"Let me take you home," Emma said.

"I need to work on a couple more things."

"I can wait."

"No, that's okay."

"How are you going to get home?" Emma asked.

"I can call Robyn," I lied.

"This late at night?"

"She doesn't mind."

"How about if I pick you up in the morning?"

"No, I will be fine."

"But your car is in the shop."

"Emma, the court is walking distance and I like to walk. I will see you at eight in the morning at the courthouse."

"Okay."

I escorted Emma out of my office. I printed extra copies of the documents and stuffed them in my briefcase. I then turned off my computer.

I walked over to my couch futon and made it into a bed. I pulled out sheets and a blanket and put them on my futon. I then took off my clothes and put on a t-shirt.

It had been a couple of months since I had lost my apartment. I needed to hit the gym at six so I could take a shower and be ready for court in the morning.

I turned off the light and said a silent prayer of thanks. Today had been a good day. Shawn was now single. We would be married in due time. Tomorrow could be even better if I won Emma's case. The contingency fee of $125,000 would pay off my bills and I would have money left over.

Chapter Twelve

April 20, 2009 6:02 a.m.

    I called the state and left a message for the state's counsel about our application for a restraining order. I hit the gym and took a shower. I squeezed into my best lawyer suit. It was a charcoal gray wool blend. A few months ago, it had fit perfectly. Now, I couldn't button the skirt and the jacket barely fit. I took a safety pin from my purse and used it to clasp my skirt closed.

    I put on a dab of make-up, combed my thick, curly hair into a ponytail, and secured it with a hairclip. I slipped on my three inch pumps.

    I glanced at myself in the mirror. I looked quite lawyerly. I was now ready to fight Emma's case and earn $125,000.

    I looked at my watch. It was 7:45 a.m. I left the gym and walked swiftly to the courthouse.

I went through the metal detector and waited for Emma. I glanced at the court's clock. It was 8:17 a.m. and Emma was not at the courthouse. Dammit, where was she? This was her day and she should be here. What if the judge asked me questions that I could not answer?

I wanted to turn away and forget about Emma and her case. But I couldn't do that. I needed to do something. I walked to the filing clerk's window and handed her documents. The filing clerk reviewed the documents and handed me a paper slip along with the documents.

"You have been assigned to Department 14. It's on the third floor," the clerk said.

I thanked the clerk. I felt someone tapping my shoulder.

I turned around and it was Emma. She was dressed in a crisp navy blue suit with matching pumps.

I wanted to chastise her for being late, but I knew better. Instead, I said, "Emma, we were assigned to Department 14."

"Do you know who the judge is?"

"No, I don't."

"Let's go then."

We boarded the elevator in silence. When the elevator's doors opened, I felt a quiver in my stomach.

I wanted to go to the women's bathroom and relax for a minute or two, but I knew that there was no time.

Emma and I walked into the courtroom side by side. I instructed Emma to sit down while I walked toward the court clerk's desk.

I handed the papers to her and the court clerk said, "I will take the papers to the judge's chambers for her review. The state's counsel is on his way. So it will be a few minutes."

"Thank you. Who is the judge for this department?"

"Judge Lynda Belkin."

"Is she a new judge?"

"No, she's been a judge for a long time. She used to be at the criminal court. Now, she's in the civil division."

"Thank you for the information."

I walked to where Emma was seated and sat down next to her.

"Emma, I found out that judge is Lynda Belkin."

Emma's eyes glazed over and her hands began to shake. "Get me assigned to someone else. She's a major bitch."

"What do you mean by that?"

"I don't trust her."

"Was she a member of the recall committee?"

"No, she's a former legal aid lawyer."

"Did she work on your campaign to oppose the recall?"

"She barely did anything. She was practically useless."

"So what did she do to you?"

"She destroyed my family."

"What do you mean by that?"

"Instead of helping me put my family back together, she let my family fall apart."

"How did she do that?"

"She wouldn't call my husband and tell him to let me come back. She wouldn't talk to my daughter. She wouldn't do anything for me."

"Why would she have an obligation to do anything?"

"Because she was my friend."

"Were you close friends?"

"She and I were roommates back in college. We went to different law schools. But we stayed in touch and Lynda was like a sister I never had."

"I'm sorry that your friendship did not work out."

"Don't be sorry. Just get that bitch off my case."

I opened my mouth to ask Emma another question, but I was interrupted by the court clerk.

"Ms. Canton, the judge would like to see you now."

I felt a twinge in my stomach and turned around to see the state's counsel.

He was a burly Latino in his mid-forties with graying hair dressed in a navy blue suit. I had seen him in the newspapers. Juan Segura was heavily involved with the San Jose community. He was an icon to many. Before joining the state, he had battled cases for immigrants that no one had wanted to take. He had won most of them.

I grabbed my briefcase and documents and headed into the judge's chambers. It was show time. With only four hours of sleep, I would try to do my best.

Chapter Thirteen

Judge Belkin was seated behind her desk. She wore a purple pantsuit that accented her three hundred pound body. Her big round face made her look younger than her sixty-something years. Her skin was pale and her eyes were a dull blue. Her lips were almost non-existent. The judge's nose was crooked and her light brown frizzy hair was shapeless.

I sat down and pulled out the papers from my briefcase. Juan Segura sat beside me.

Judge Belkin looked at me and said, "Ms. Canton, I have read your petition. You present an interesting set of facts."

"Your honor before I go into the merits of the application for the restraining order, petitioner requests that this court is recused from her case," I said.

"On what ground?" Judge Belkin asked.

"Your honor, petitioner believes that this court cannot be fair and impartial in her case."

"Objection," Juan said. "The state has been given no notice of this motion. The court should deny this motion on the basis that it is untimely."

"Your honor, the statute does not require that we provide notice. We just filed our ex parte application about twenty minutes ago and petitioner informed me about the conflict a few minutes ago. Her future is a stake. A 73 million dollar lottery ticket will expire today."

Judge Belkin stared at me with a stern expression. "Given that time is the essence in this matter, the court will hear petitioner's motion for recusal."

"Your honor, as a matter law, petitioner is entitled to one peremptory challenge in which the court is required to remove itself," I argued. "The form for the challenge is online and petitioner is prepared to complete it. At this time, we are asking for a five-minute recess to complete the said form and submit to the court.

"Objection your honor," Juan said. "Two weeks ago, the California Supreme Court struck down the peremptory challenge section of the statute on the basis that it was overbroad in its scope. The form is no longer valid. Furthermore, the court held that a party seeking to recuse a judge must present arguments for her motion for recusal before the said judge or presiding judge."

I responded, "Your honor, at this time we ask that our motion be removed to the presiding judge of this court in order that a fair and impartial decision can be rendered."

"Objection is denied," Judge Belkin responded. "Ms. Canton, present your argument."

"Yes, your honor," I responded. "The petitioner is a former judge of this court. Twenty-three years ago, she was recalled. She told me that you worked on her campaign opposing the recall. As a result, petitioner is very concerned about whether you can be fair and impartial. Our first question to the court is the following: What was your role in the recall campaign?"

"Objection," Juan responded. "Petitioner's counsel does not have the right to cross-examine this court."

"Your honor, the statute clearly gives us this right. There is ample case law that supports a party has the right to cross-examine a judge. Unless the court ruled on this issue, the cross-examination should proceed."

Judge Belkin turned to Juan and said, "Did the California Supreme Court make a determination on this issue?"

"No, it did not your honor," Juan responded. "However, in a separate case, an Alameda County Superior Court judge refused to allow a party to cross-examine the court on the grounds that it violated the state constitution."

"Was this decision supported by the Court of Appeals or the California Supreme Court?" Judge Belkin asked.

"Your honor, there were oral arguments presented before the Court of Appeals a few weeks ago," Juan said. "A decision is expected to be issued in the next month or two."

"This court is not bound to follow another superior court judge's ruling," I argued. "It is clearly not precedent and the Court of Appeals has not made a decision. On the other hand, ample case law supports my argument."

"Cross examination may proceed," Judge Belkin responded.

"Thank you your honor," I said. "Your honor, again the petitioner asks: What was your role in the recall campaign?"

Judge Belkin put her hands on her desk. She looked at me directly in the eyes. "I was an impartial observer at a public meeting. I did not represent your client or her campaign at that meeting."

"Your honor, my client's memory differs from yours."

"Ms. Canton, are you suggesting that this court is not factual in its response?"

"There are two different set of facts. Sometimes memories fade and what we remember may not represent what in actually happened at the time."

"Counsel, I suggest that you move on. You are not making a good impression with this court."

"My client also has informed me that you have a long standing relationship with her. Back in college, you and she were best friends and your friendship continued when you departed for different law schools."

"Counsel, petitioner and I shared a suite with six other women in college during our sophomore year. I hardly associated with her. While I would study countless hours on a daily basis, she was active in her social life. We had nothing in common."

"So you and my client were never friends."

Judge Belkin stared at me as if she wanted to reprimand me. "No, we were not. We were simply two students in the same living quarters."

"Didn't you and the petitioner stay in touch with each other after you left for law school?" I asked.

The pupils of Judge Belkin's eyes enlarged. "No, there was no effort on my part. We perhaps ran into each other two or three times during our summers off from law school."

"What about after law school?"

"We rarely spoke."

"Were you a judge when she was on the bench?"

"No, I was not. I was appointed five years after she had been recalled."

"My client's memory is a lot different from the court's," I said boldly.

"Counsel, do you have anything else that you would like to add?"

"No, I do not."

"Mr. Segura, does the state have any response?"

Juan touched his brow lightly. "The state feels that this motion is without merit and therefore asks the court to deny it."

Judge Belkin tapped her left hand slightly and exhaled. "The court has heard petitioner's motion for recusal. Petitioner has failed to show that the court cannot be fair and impartial. Accordingly, petitioner's motion is hereby denied."

"Your honor, the petitioner asks that you reconsider your decision. Petitioner would like to testify."

"Denied."

Judge Belkin's word "denied" echoed in my mind. Emma would not be happy. In fact, she would be pissed.

I stared at the clock in her chambers. It was already 8:50 a.m. I felt a pain in my lower pelvis. Cramps. This was the worst time for my period to start. Why now?

"Counsel, now that we have disposed of your motion, the court will need to examine petitioner's application for the restraining order."

"Your honor, may I defer argument for five minutes?"

"On what ground?"

"I need to go to the bathroom."

"Can't you wait? You're not in grade school."

Gayle Tiller

"I have cramps and I really need to go."

"Five minutes. Back in my chambers at 8:55 and not a minute later."

Chapter Fourteen

When I walked out of the judge's chambers, Emma greeted me.

"Did we get rid of her?" Emma asked with a smile.

"Emma let's not discuss your case here. I have to go to the bathroom."

Emma nodded and followed me. We walked in silence together.

Once outside the courtroom's door, I took a deep breath and said, "She denied our motion for recusal."

Emma's face became twisted. "What the hell happened in there?"

I told Emma the reasons for the judge's decision.

"She's a lying bitch."

"She made the decision and I can't change it. I still need to go back and argue the application for the restraining order."

"Can't you appeal the motion?"

"Emma, there's no time. Your lottery ticket expires today. We need to focus on the restraining order."

"Is she still big as a house?"

I nodded my head.

"Back in college, that fat ass bitch would eat more than a team of football players. You would think that big bitch would have been dead from a heart attack by now."

I wanted to tell Emma to refrain from calling the judge a "bitch" and "fat." Instead, I said nothing, because it was pointless.

"I have three minutes to use the bathroom and get back to the judge's chambers," I said.

"That should be long enough," Emma responded.

"I have cramps."

"Thank God, I don't have to deal with that anymore. Menopause is the best thing that ever happened to me."

"I have something to look forward to," I mumbled.

I left Emma standing in the hall, went into the bathroom and used the facilities. I then washed my hands and walked out of the bathroom.

"Are you feeling better?" Emma asked.

"Yes," I lied.

"Are we going to win?"

"I will give it my best."

Emma's face dropped. "Tell me that we are going to win."

"Emma, like I said before I will give it 100 percent."

"That's not good enough."

"I have one minute to be in the judge's chambers."

"Give me your left hand."

"Why?"

"Just do it."

I moved my left hand toward Emma. She took my hand and put a shapeless small violet and black speckled rock inside it.

"What is this?"

"It's a lucky charm."

"Does it work?"

Emma looked at me as if I had asked her a stupid question. She answered, "Of course, it does. I had the charm when my daughter was born and when I was elected as a judge."

"What about when you were recalled?"

Emma's face turned red. "I had lost the charm. I didn't find it again until a few months ago. This was right before I bought the lottery ticket."

"Okay."

"Dianne, you need to keep the charm in your left pocket during your argument. It will help us."

With thirty seconds left before I was due back in the judge's chambers, I didn't have time to argue with Emma. I wasn't superstitious and I barely read my horoscope. When I did, it was never accurate.

I nodded my head and rubbed the charm a bit. I inserted it in my left suit pocket. I left Emma in the hallway and walked into the courtroom.

Now was show time. I hoped that we would get what Emma wanted.

Chapter Fifteen

I glanced at my watch before I walked into Judge Belkin's chambers. It was exactly 8:56. I was a minute past the judge's deadline.

Judge Belkin wore a slight scowl on her face. Opposing counsel fiddled with papers in his briefcase. I took a seat next to him and took out the application for the restraining order from my briefcase.

Judge Belkin clasped her hands and placed them firmly on her desk. "Ms. Canton, five minutes means five minutes. You went over the time allotted and this is totally unacceptable."

I felt the heat rising in my face. I lowered my head slightly. "I am truly sorry. It will not happen again."

"If it happens again, the court will hold you in contempt."

"Understood."

"Good. Now Ms. Canton, please state your case."

"Your honor, petitioner is hereby asking that the court issue a restraining order that orders the Lottery Authority to not publicly release her name as a winner of the $73 million lottery prize. She is requesting this order on the following ground. Petitioner will suffer irreparable harm if she is named as the winner. Petitioner is a former judge who was recalled twenty-three years ago.

"During the campaign, she was thoroughly humiliated. Petitioner's opponents blamed her for the death of a San Jose State cheerleader. Prior to her death, petitioner had presided over a case in which the alleged killer had been arrested illegally. When petitioner found that there were no grounds to hold him, petitioner released him.

"A few weeks later, the cheerleader was killed. The reality was that she was killed, because of a bad drug deal. This was not brought out in the media. Instead, there was a huge cover-up.

"A few months after the recall election, petitioner received a letter telling her that the real reason for the recall was to launder drug money. Over a million dollars was laundered through the recall committee. Phony contributions were made and phony expenses were paid out. It was the perfect operation.

"Yesterday evening, petitioner obtained a copy of the recall campaign report from the Santa Clara County Registrar of Voters. To her surprise, a white correction fluid obscured the names of the major contributors and expenditures. Petitioner believes they were covered up in order to hide the money laundering operation.

"And until recently, petitioner received death threats and hang up calls from unknown sources. It was only a few months ago, the calls suddenly stopped.

"Petitioner's fear is that if her name is publicly released, reporters will swarm around her like the paparazzi. She will be publicly mocked and the death threats will resume. Petitioner's life is at stake and the public clearly has an interest in preserving life. Therefore, petitioner respectfully requests that the court restrain the state from releasing her name."

Juan shook his head. "In her declaration, petitioner admits that she has no idea when the contributors' and vendors' names were covered up by this so-called correction fluid. For all we know this could have happened quite recently. Someone may have accidentally spilled white fluid on the report. And there is no indication whatsoever that she did not have access to the report during her recall election or even after. Accordingly, her conspiracy theory is not supported by any evidence.

"More importantly, petitioner alleges that she received death threats over a period of more than twenty years. Yet, she never applied once to this court for a restraining order. Nor did she ever contact the San Jose Police Department for an investigation. She failed to do anything until the day her lottery ticket is set to expire. Her claims lack credibility and fail to show that she will suffer irreparable harm.

"Moreover, what petitioner has failed to address is the public's right to know about who wins the lottery. We all have heard of reality TV. There are countless examples of winners who have less than a perfect past. Criminal histories and past affairs give reality TV high ratings. An average Jane or Joe is just too boring. The same is true here. A recalled judge won't just be a great news story. It may spark an unprecedented interest in the lottery. More people will buy lottery tickets. This will increase the revenues that go to our schools and our children will be the winners in the end. Accordingly, it is in the public's interest that petitioner's name is publicized."

I clasped my hands. "Your honor, the court has the discretion to hear petitioner's testimony. It is our firm belief that such testimony will show that petitioner had bona fide reasons not to pursue her legal rights until now. More importantly, because her life is at stake, it is only fair and equitable that she should be allowed to testify."

Juan argued, "Your honor, the state objects. The application has been made and such reasons should have been included. Moreover, the public again has an overriding interest to know the name of the winner of the lottery. By granting a restraining order, the lottery will lose its transparency and the public could lose faith. Lottery sales could plummet and in the end, our schools and children will be hurt. The state in good conscience cannot allow this to happen."

I put my hands on Judge Belkin's desk. "Petitioner is an innocent woman who faces the loss of life if her name is publicized," I said. "The fact that such additional facts petitioner could have provided through her testimony was not included in her application is immaterial. What really matters is that her testimony shall show that her life should be protected and the restraining order is the only means to do this. The public certainly values life over death."

Judge Belkin fumed, "The court has heard enough. The application itself is very poorly written and convoluted. It clearly does not rise to the standard of granting a restraining order.

"However, with the arguments presented by petitioner's counsel, it is clear that the court cannot in good conscience deny a restraining order without hearing additional facts. Accordingly, the court is hereby permitting the testimony of petitioner."

Judge Belkin looked at me directly in the eyes. "Ms. Canton, please return to the court's chambers in ten minutes with petitioner."

I suppressed a smile in order to look somber. "Your honor, petitioner would like a court reporter present for her testimony."

"The court denies your request," Judge Belkin responded.

"On what ground?" I asked.

"Ms. Canton, before the court changes its ruling about petitioner's testimony, please refrain further questions about the court reporter."

"Understood."

I got up to leave my chair. If we were lucky, Emma's testimony would be enough for the judge to grant the restraining order. If not, I would have to deal with Emma's wrath.

Chapter Sixteen

I walked out of the judge's chambers. I made a motion to Emma to follow me outside the courtroom. I then told Emma what had happened.

Emma scoffed, "That fat cow should have granted the restraining order. There's no reason for me to testify."

"Emma, if you don't testify, you can forget about us getting it."

Emma rolled her eyes and said, "Yeah, I'll do it. But that fat ass bitch needs to stop trying to hurt me."

I ignored Emma's comment. I said firmly, "I want you on your best behavior in the judge's chambers. If you say one derogatory comment about her, I will walk out and I will not look back."

"You wouldn't do that."

"This is a serious matter and you need to act appropriately. I don't have time to deal with rude behavior."

Emma protested, "Young lady, you need to stop treating me like a child. I'm old enough to be your mother."

"Then start acting like it."

Emma's shoulders hunched slightly and she looked as though I had slapped her face. "Okay," she mumbled.

We quickly went over Emma's testimony. I then glanced at my watch. I beckoned Emma to follow me.

We walked side by side into the judge's chambers. We sat next to Juan. Judge Belkin was behind her desk with a stern expression on her face.

Emma smiled. "Lynda, it's so good to see you."

Judge Belkin said coldly, "Ms. Watkins, it's Judge Belkin."

Emma's face turned red. "Don't we have . . ."

I interrupted Emma and said, "Judge Belkin, I want to thank the court for allowing petitioner to testify."

Judge Belkin replied, "You're welcome." She turned to Emma and administered the court's oath.

"Ms. Canton, you now may question petitioner."

"Ms. Watkins, please provide your work history."

"I had practiced law for almost twelve years before I was appointed as a judge to this court. I served on this court for six years. During my tenure, there was a recall election. I lost the election and lost my judgeship. After that, I worked for a nonprofit for twenty years. I am now retired."

"Why were you recalled?"

"My opponents blamed me for a San Jose State cheerleader's death. The reality was that I had simply done my job by following the constitution," Emma responded.

"What do you mean by that?" I asked.

"Her alleged killer had appeared in my courtroom prior to her death. He had been brought in on a case in which his fourth amendment rights had been violated. I had no choice but to release him. A few weeks later, he allegedly killed a San Jose State cheerleader."

"Do you know the circumstances of the alleged victim's death?" I asked.

"I heard from close sources that she was a drug addict and the deal went bad."

Juan interrupted, "Objection, hearsay."

Judge Belkin said, "Objection sustained."

"Ms. Watkins, do you think you were unfairly targeted for the recall?"

"Absolutely. Again, I had simply followed the constitution."

"But the voters did not think so."

"Apparently not, because I lost by a huge landslide. 75 percent voted for the recall."

"Was this the only reason for the recall?"

"Near the end of my campaign, they totally destroyed me and my family."

"What do you mean by that?"

"They published excerpts from a letter that I had written to my lover on the front page of the newspaper."

"So you are saying that if the letter had not been published, you might be still in office."

"There is a double standard in this country. If I had been a man, no one would have blinked an eye."

Juan raised his right hand and said, "Objection, calls for speculation."

Judge Belkin replied, "Objection sustained."

"Ms. Watkins, your family life was destroyed by the exposure of your affair and you were unfairly blamed for the death of the San Jose State cheerleader. However, all this has been publicized in the media. Given this, why don't you want your name released now? The harm has already been done."

"Because I found out after the election the real reason why I was recalled; it had nothing to do with the girl's death. Instead, the real reason had to do with the fact that the recall committee was used as a ruse to launder drug money. Apparently, this was a practice used not only in this county but other counties as well."

"Ms. Watkins, who told you about the reason?"

"A source."

"Who was the source?"

"I don't know. I received an anonymous letter a few months after the election."

"Do you have this letter?"

"Unfortunately, I do not."

"Did you discard it?"

"I may have thrown it away by mistake. Or it could be buried in my papers," Emma answered while folding her arms.

"Is there a reason why you didn't keep the letter in a safe place?" I asked.

"After the election, I gave up on life," Emma said while lowering her head. "I would medicate myself with alcohol until I would fall asleep. When I moved into senior housing two years ago, I threw away a lot of things. I don't know if I disposed of the letter by mistake."

"Ms. Watkins, when did you obtain the campaign recall report?"

"Last night."

"What did the report show?"

Juan roared, "Objection, calls for expert testimony."

Judge Belkin replied, "Objection sustained."

"Ms. Watkins, the recall election occurred twenty-three years ago, so what is the danger of releasing your name now?"

"For over twenty years, I received hang up calls and there were also death threats. They knew I found out the real reason of the recall."

"Did you go to the police?"

"The police. Absolutely not. I could not trust them."

"The calls stopped a few months ago. So what is the problem with releasing your name now?"

"Because now they will see that I am back in the limelight. They will not only drudge up the past, but they also may start the hang up calls and death threats."

"The death threats?"

"They told me that if I ever went public with the information I could forget about seeing the light of day again."

"What does that mean?"

Juan said, "Objection, calls for speculation."

Judge Belkin replied, "Objection overruled."

"Ms. Watkins, please answer the question," I said gently.

Emma stared directly at Judge Belkin. "To me, it meant I could lose my life."

"How?" I asked.

"I am afraid that I could be murdered," Emma answered.

"I have no further questions," I said.

Chapter Seventeen

Juan put his hands firmly in front of him and turned to Emma. "Ms. Watkins, how long have you had the lottery ticket?"

"180 days."

"Isn't today the last day that you can turn the lottery ticket in?"

I said, "Objection, calls for a legal conclusion."

Judge Belkin replied, "Objection sustained."

Juan tugged at his tie. "Ms. Watkins, you mentioned that you received threatening calls after the election."

"That is correct."

"Did you tape record the threats?" he asked.

"No," Emma answered.

"Did you keep a diary about the threats?"

"No," Emma answered.

"Did you tell anyone about the threats?"

"I told one close friend."

"What is his or her name?"

"Elena Shopely."

"Was she another judge?" Juan asked.

"No. She was a friend I met in rehab."

"Are you still in touch with her?" Juan asked.

"No," Emma answered.

"Why is that?"

"She died from cirrhosis of the liver about five years ago."

"When you received the threats had you been drinking?"

"I really don't remember."

"So during the threats, it is possible you could have been drinking?"

"Like I said I don't remember."

"Ms. Watkins, have you ever had a hallucination?"

"I don't think so."

"So it's possible that you've had a hallucination?"

"I'm not crazy," Emma answered as she folded her arms and looked at Juan directly in the eyes.

"Ms. Watkins, please answer my question. Is it possible you've had a hallucination?"

"Anything is possible."

"So you may have had one?"

"Maybe."

"Is it possible that you had a hallucination about the threats?"

"I am a sane woman and I've never been diagnosed with any mental illness."

Juan turned to Judge Belkin and said, "Your honor, at this time, the state asks the witness be instructed to answer the question."

Judge Belkin glared at Emma and said, "Ms. Watkins, answer the question."

"What was the question?" Emma asked.

"Ms. Watkins, is it possible that you had a hallucination about the threats?" Juan asked.

"It's highly unlikely," Emma responded.

"So it's a possibility," Juan said.

"I don't know," Emma responded.

"Ms. Watkins, you told the court that you never recorded the threats, you never went to the police, you never kept a diary and the only one friend you told is dead, so is it possible that the threats were simply hallucinations?"

I bellowed, "Objection, asked and answered."

Judge Belkin replied, "Objection overruled."

"Ms. Watkins, answer the question."

"It's possible but not likely," Emma answered.

"I have no further questions for Ms. Watkins."

Chapter Eighteen

I tapped my notepad and turned to Judge Belkin. "Your honor, because petitioner presented oral testimony after we made our original closing argument, we'd like the opportunity to amend it."

"Denied," Judge Belkin snapped. "Additional closing arguments by either petitioner or the state are unnecessary."

Emma's face fell. She took my notepad from my hand and wrote: *Stupid fat ass bitch.*

I glared at Emma. I pried the notepad from her and scribbled out what she had written.

Judge Belkin folded her arms and stared at us. "Ms. Canton, please control your client. The court will not tolerate such childish behavior."

"Yes, your honor," I said while bowing my head.

Judge Belkin unlocked her hands and put them firmly on her desk. "The state has a compelling interest in publicizing the names of the winners of the lottery. Media publicity helps ensure that residents will have a motive to play the lottery. There is no better advertising tool than showing a real person who has won the lottery. This will increase the number of people who play. Our schools consequently will see more revenue from the lottery. This helps our children and California as a whole.

"However, in this case, we must also consider whether the release of petitioner's name will cause her irreparable harm. Petitioner has testified that in the past her life was threatened after she learned the alleged real reason for the recall effort. She also presented evidence that the major contributors and vendors associated with the recall effort were obscured by a white thickened liquid on the political campaign report that is housed in Santa Clara County Registrar of Voters' office.

"However, there is a possibility that the threats were in fact hallucinations that may have occurred during petitioner's bouts of drinking. In addition, there is the possibility that someone accidently spilled a white liquid on the campaign report.

"Given that the facts in the case are clearly disputed, the court cannot render a decision at this time until it receives additional evidence. Accordingly, the court is hereby ordering that petitioner obtain a certified copy of the campaign report for the recall election from the Secretary of State in Sacramento and present this report in the court's chambers by 4:00 this afternoon."

I suppressed a smile and said, "Your honor, petitioner requests that she have permission to present the court with a fax of a certified copy of the campaign report under the best evidence rule."

"Request denied," Judge Belkin responded. "A facsimile is not acceptable."

"Petitioner requests that the state have the burden of producing the campaign report, because it is warehoused at a state agency," I said.

"Request denied," Judge Belkin retorted. "Petitioner is the moving party and she has the burden of producing such evidence."

"Your honor, petitioner has no further requests," I said. "We will return at 4:00."

"And not one minute later," Judge Belkin admonished. "If you are late, the court will deny your petition without any further consideration."

"Understood," I said.

"Good," Judge Belkin said while placing her hands in front of her.

I motioned Emma to get up. We walked out of the judge's chambers in silence side by side. When we were outside of the courtroom, I looked at my watch and said, "It's almost 10:00. We need to call Robyn and ask her to borrow her car."

"Why can't we drive to Sacramento in my car?" Emma asked while straightening her skirt.

"Emma, your car is not going to make a 240 mile roundtrip. It's too old. I don't want to risk it breaking down."

"My car is in great condition. We can drive it to Sacramento," Emma protested.

"Emma, $73 million is at stake. If you want to drive in your car, we can. Don't blame me if we get stuck on the freeway and we lose the one chance to win your case."

"Okay," Emma replied.

I retrieved my cell phone from my purse and dialed Robyn's phone number. To my disappointment, she did not pick up her phone. I left her a message.

"Robyn is not in. Maybe we can rent a car with your credit card," I said.

"Why can't you charge it to your credit card?" Emma asked.

"Emma, this is an expense related to your case," I protested. "Per our agreement, you are responsible for paying for it in advance. As a result, you should charge it to your credit card."

"I don't believe in credit cards," Emma winced. "They are the cause of the downfall of our economy. I have never owned one. So you will need to charge the rental to your credit card. I can pay you back when I get my social security check."

My credit card? All my credit cards were maxed out except for one. That card only had about hundred dollars left in credit and that was not enough for a car rental.

"Emma, our agreement made it clear that I would not advance any costs. That includes any credit card charges," I responded.

"Can't you make an exception?" Emma asked.

"No," I replied.

"When will your car be ready?" Emma asked. "Hasn't it been in the shop for a while?"

"Not until next week," I lied.

"What's wrong with it?"

I wanted to say it had been repossessed, but Emma did not need to know that. Instead, I said, "It's real complicated. I really don't understand cars."

"I didn't either until I took a class at San Jose City College on mechanics. You should take it."

"I will think about it," I said.

"Since you won't use your credit card, maybe we can find a place that accepts cash for deposit," Emma said.

"Do you know anyone?" I asked.

"I used to, but they shut down a few years ago," Emma replied.

"When we get back to my office, we can search for one on the Internet."

"Great. So you will front the cash."

"No," I responded.

"How are we going to pay for the rental? I don't have any money."

"Emma, I already told you I am not going to pay for it."

"Can't we use the five hundred dollars I gave you yesterday?" Emma asked.

"No."

"We won't rent out the car," Emma snapped.

"Emma, you must have some other money," I pleaded.

Emma shook her head. "I have $50.00 in my checking account and that needs to last until next month."

"What about savings?" I asked.

"I don't have a savings account," Emma responded.

"Do you have any cash at home?" I asked.

"I have about ten or fifteen dollars in quarters for my laundry," Emma replied.

"Any savings bonds?" I asked.

"I forgot about my savings bonds," Emma responded as her face brightened. "I have a few."

"How much are they worth?"

"I don't know. They're in my security box at my bank."

"Let's go to your bank and cash them. So we will have enough for the deposit."

"Okay," Emma said as she nodded her head.

Emma and I walked in silence until we found Emma's battered car on the street. Emma unlocked the doors and then we got into it. It took a minute or two before the car started. Emma drove a few blocks until we found the freeway to her bank.

Chapter Nineteen

When we arrived at Emma's bank, a woman in her late thirties, who was clad in an ugly tan suit that emphasized her rolls of fat on her back and belly, stopped us at the door. Her bare pale legs were lined with twisted blue and purple veins.

"We have an ATM outside," she said as she pointed. "It allows you to take care of everything you need."

"Does it cash savings bonds?" I asked.

"No, it doesn't," she faltered. "You'll need to do that in here. I can help you out with that."

"We'll need to get the savings bonds from her security box."

"And who are you?" the bank worker asked as she looked at me up and down.

"I'm her lawyer."

"Okay. I will need to see some identification from the customer."

Emma flashed her driver's license. The bank worker beckoned us to follow her. She got out her key and unlocked the security vault. We followed her down a dimly lit hallway until we reached Emma's security box. Emma retrieved her key and took out the box.

The box showed a stack of bonds. Emma carefully counted the bonds. There was $1,250.00 in EE bonds. That meant that they were worth at least half of that. I felt relieved. That would be more than enough to rent a car.

Emma put the bonds in her purse. We walked back to the main lobby of the bank.

The bank worker sat us down at her desk. With the exception of a computer and the nameplate, the desk was barren.

She handed a form for Emma to complete. Emma filled it out and gave it back to her.

"Let's see the bonds."

Emma handed her the bonds.

She punched in the bonds' numbers in her computer and turned to Emma.

"Most of your bonds were purchased less than a year ago. You have to hold the bonds for at least a year before you can cash them."

"That's not true. The rule is six months. The last bond I bought was over seven months ago," Emma replied in a slightly irritated tone.

"The rule changed back in 2003."

"2003? That was six years ago," Emma scowled. "Your tellers never told me that when I bought the bonds."

"Our tellers don't have that responsibility. You should have known the information."

"How?"

"Ma'am, it's on the government web site for bonds."

"No one ever told me about it," Emma scoffed.

"If you had googled it, you would have found it."

Emma looked the bank clerk up and down. "It's too bad, no one ever told you there are web sites for weight loss and vein surgery."

The bank worker's face turned red. "Regardless, we cannot cash bonds that were purchased less than a year ago."

I interjected, "We understand your constraints. We will cash the remaining bonds."

"Okay," she said while punching in numbers into her computer. "Those bonds currently have a cash value of $318.53."

"That can't be right," Emma protested.

24 Hour Lottery Ticket

"It's correct," the worker responded. "Do you want to cash the bonds?"

"Yes. Just give me the cash right now," Emma said angrily.

"I'll be back in a couple minutes. I'll need to get the money." She got up and walked to the teller line.

Once the bank worker was out of ear range, I said, "You need to stop being rude to people."

"Rude? She was rude to me. I was telling her the truth. She needs to do something about those ugly veins. At least, wear pantyhose."

"Emma, women don't wear pantyhose anymore."

"You mean younger women don't. It's plain stupid when you have ugly legs. And those fat ass rolls on her are enough to make sausages. And hell, if you don't start dieting, you're going to look like her."

"Emma, that's enough," I said while glaring at her. "From now on I want you to be nice. I don't care about how ugly her legs are or how unattractive her rolls are. Being mean won't get us anywhere."

"Hell, being nice wouldn't have changed anything. She still wasn't going to let me cash all of my bonds."

"Emma, I am not going to spend my day with a rude person," I said. "I am going the extra mile for you and I expect your full cooperation."

"Understood," Emma responded.

We waited in silence for a few minutes until the bank worker returned to her desk. She handed the money to Emma.

"Is there anything else that I can help you with?" she asked.

"Yes, put a sign on your wall about the rule change," Emma replied.

"We will forward your suggestion to our corporate headquarters," the worker responded.

"Thank you," Emma said.

"Yes, thank you for your time. We really appreciate it," I said.

Emma and I got up and headed to the street.

Chapter Twenty

Emma and I stopped at my office briefly. Through an online search, we found a car rental dealer that gave a free gas refill and accepted $300.00 cash for a deposit. I printed out the ad.

I unlocked the top drawer of my desk and retrieved my good credit card that had about $100 left in available credit. I stuffed the credit card in my purse and relocked my desk. From my tiny office refrigerator, I grabbed yogurt and fruit and put the items in a bag with plastic spoons.

Emma and I left my office and drove to the car rental place. It was on the Eastside at Story and King located in a strip mall. Most of the stores had signs written in Spanish. The car rental dealer had a sign that was written in English, Spanish and Vietnamese.

A paunchy Latina in her late fifties greeted us. She had short, cropped, salt and pepper hair with a few scattered wrinkles on her face.

"We'd like to rent a car today," I said.

"Where are you going?" she asked.

"To Sacramento," I replied.

"My nephew goes to Sacramento State," the clerk said.

"I heard it's a good school," I said.

"So how long will you and your mother need the car?" the clerk asked.

Emma glared at the clerk. It was obvious that the word "mother" did not resonate with her. However, I was not interested in correcting the clerk's mistake.

"We will need it for a day," I said. "We will return it tomorrow."

"Okay. What type of car do you want?" the clerk asked.

"The most affordable one you have," I replied.

The woman showed us a few different cars and we settled on a Honda Civic. We then went inside the car rental office.

"How will you be paying?" the clerk asked.

"By cash," Emma replied.

"The deposit is $300.00 and that includes a free gas refill. With tax, that will be $327.75."

Emma opened her purse and handed her the money.

"Ma'am, you only gave me $318.53," the clerk said. "You're short by $9.22."

"This is all I have," Emma replied.

I nudged Emma and asked, "Where's the change I gave you this morning?"

"I left it at home," Emma responded.

"I can't rent the car unless I have the full amount," the clerk said.

I pulled out the Internet ad and flashed it. "It says you will rent a car for $300.00 cash deposit."

The clerk grabbed the paper from my hand. "Robert, our webmaster forgot to include the tax part."

"Since your ad did not include it, we don't need to pay the tax," I countered.

"Look, I don't care what the ad says. I am not renting the car without $9.22."

"This is false advertising and if you don't rent us the car, we will report you to the Board of Consumer Affairs," I said.

"Go ahead," the clerk replied.

I was surprised by the clerk's stubbornness. I needed to think fast or we would never get to Sacramento. "We don't have cash. But we can offer something else."

"Like what?" the clerk asked.

"How about a free legal consultation?"

The clerk peered at me suspiciously. "Are you a lawyer?"

"Yes," I answered.

"What kind of lawyer doesn't have ten bucks on her?" the clerk smirked.

"Ma'am, I am offering a free consultation. You never know when you'll need legal advice."

"Lady, I don't need some broke ass lawyer. I need a good one."

Emma's eyes widened and her face turned a bright red. "Don't insult my lawyer. She's one of the best."

"You're her mother. So of course, you would say something like that," the clerk sneered.

"I'm not her mother," Emma responded. "I am no more related to her than you are."

"My son is a lawyer and he always has cash on him. So if I need help, I can go to him," the clerk scoffed.

"Do you like to read?" Emma asked.

"Why? Are you an author?"

"No, but I dabble in poetry."

"I'm not into poetry. Novels are my thing."

"Fiction is good for the soul." Emma opened her purse and handed a gift card to the woman. "It's worth ten dollars and you can use it in any bookstore."

"Just because the card says ten dollars doesn't mean that it hasn't already been used."

"Call the 800 number on the back of the card."

The clerk dialed the phone number and verified the gift card.

"I will accept the gift card in lieu of cash. However, the card will not be returned."

"That's fine," Emma said.

Emma completed the paperwork for the car.

"By the way, what are you going to Sacramento for?"

"It's personal," Emma replied.

"If it's personal, why are you taking your lawyer with you?"

"It's none of your business," Emma answered.

The clerk handed Emma the keys and pointed outside to the car. "Wait until my son hears about you two."

When we got to our rental car, Emma said, "Stupid bitch."

I wanted to say I agreed. Instead, I glanced at my watch and said, "It will take an hour and forty minutes to get to Sacramento. Let me drive."

Emma handed me the keys and we got into the car. I turned on the engine. Finally, we were on our way.

Chapter Twenty-one

We were about halfway to Sacramento when Emma said, "I have to pee."

I looked for a rest stop sign. "The next bathroom is ten miles. So we'll be there in a few minutes."

"I can't wait that long," Emma whined.

"You'll have to. There's nowhere else to go."

"I need to go now."

"Emma, just be patient, we'll be there in no time."

"If we don't find a place soon, I will pee in the car," Emma snapped.

"There is no way in hell you're going to ruin this car," I said. "You will wait."

"I have a weak bladder," Emma said. "It started with menopause. There's nothing I can do about it."

"Do you wear diapers?" I asked.

"For Christ's sake, I'm not an invalid," Emma hissed. "Diapers are for old people."

I gritted my teeth. "If you wore diapers, you could pee. Now, you're just going to have to hold it."

"Dammit, I have to go now. I have one more minute until I'm not going to have a choice."

I peered out the window. There were no bushes -- just concrete. "Emma, we'll be at the bathroom in about five minutes."

"Pull over now. I have to go."

"I can't. There's nowhere for you to pee."

Emma's face turned red. "Dianne, I told you to pull over."

"You need to wait," I shouted.

"No," Emma yelled. She lunged for the steering wheel and tried to pry it from my hands.

"What the hell are you doing? You're going to get us in an accident."

Emma would not release the steering wheel. "If you don't pull over now, I am going to pee right now or wreck the car."

"Emma, just let go of the steering wheel," I demanded.

"Not unless you pull over now," Emma responded.

"Fine," I said. Emma released her grip as I veered to the emergency lane.

Emma jumped out of the car and pulled off her panties and pantyhose in one swoop and lifted her skirt. I turned my head as she did her business.

"Do you have tissue?" she asked.

I nodded my head. I searched my purse and handed her a wad. She then wiped herself and pulled down her skirt.

"Do you feel better?" I asked.

"Yeah," she said.

Emma opened the passenger door to get back into the car. I turned on the ignition. I glanced at my rearview mirror. To my surprise, a California Highway Patrol car had just pulled up behind us.

The officer walked out of his car. He was forty-something with a body that screamed steroids. "Are you ladies okay?" he asked.

"Officer, we just had to pull over for a bit," I replied. "We are leaving now."

"I received a report about a senior citizen lady urinating on the side of the road," the officer said.

Emma's face turned red. "I am not a senior citizen. I am a vibrant middle-aged woman."

"Ma'am, so did you urinate on the highway just now?"

"Officer, if I were a man, would you ask me that?"

"Ma'am, men and women are built differently."

"That's sexism," Emma protested.

"No, it's not. It's reality," the officer responded.

"Do you know it's illegal to treat people differently based on gender?" Emma asked.

"Ma'am, of course I do," the officer responded.

"Then I suggest if you want to avoid a lawsuit, you stop asking women whether they peed on the side of the road," Emma said. "If men can do it, so can women."

"Are you a feminist?" the officer asked.

"Absolutely and proud of it," Emma smirked.

"My ex's mother was one and it broke up our marriage."

"Officer, we don't have time to analyze your marriage. We're on deadline and we need to go to Sacramento," Emma said.

"Why are you going to Sacramento?" the officer asked.

"I can't tell you," Emma responded.

"Why not?" the officer asked.

I interjected, "Officer, I'm an attorney and this is a confidential matter. We really need to leave and time is of the essence. We need to be back in San Jose later this afternoon."

"You two can go." The officer turned to Emma. "Ma'am, the next time you go on a trip, go to the bathroom first."

Emma nodded her head as the officer walked back to his car. Once the officer was in his car, Emma muttered, "Asshole."

I said nothing. I turned on the ignition and started driving.

Chapter Twenty-two

Emma turned to me in the car and put her hand on my shoulder.

"How far are we from Sacramento?" she asked.

"About twenty minutes," I answered.

She stared at me for a few seconds and said, "You both have those intense green eyes."

"Your law clerk and I have the same color eyes. That's interesting," I mused.

"No, not Brad," she responded.

"Then who?" I asked.

"Your father," she replied.

The word "father" echoed in my head for a few seconds. I felt a gnawing pain in my stomach. I wanted to pull over. Instead, I kept driving and said nothing. I then flashed back to when I was six years old.

My mother was sitting next to the kitchen table in our studio apartment. She had the job section of the newspaper spread out.

When she looked up, she was startled when she saw my black eye. "Oh my lord," she exclaimed. "Who hurt you?"

"It was that nigger girl," I replied.

My mother's face turned red. "What did you say?"

"The nigger girl Judy did it," I said.

My mother got up from her chair and slapped me hard. "Don't ever say that word again."

Tears ran down my face. "Mommy, I'm sorry but I didn't do anything wrong."

My mother took me into her arms. "I'm sorry that I hit you. But the n-word is a bad word."

"I won't say it again," I said. "But Judy punched me in the eye."

"Why did she do that?" my mother asked.

"Because I hit her," I replied.

"Why?" my mother asked.

"She said that I was black like her. I told her I wasn't. She then kept calling me black so I hit her."

24 Hour Lottery Ticket

My mother put her arms around me. "Dianne, there's nothing wrong with being black. Your father is black."

"Mommy, I don't have a father," I said.

"Yes, you do," she said. "He's a black man. That means that you're black also."

"I don't want to be black," I cried. "I'm white."

My mother shook me hard. "Don't argue with me. You're black."

My mother walked to the closet and took out a small box. She opened it and retrieved a faded black and white picture of a light-skinned African-American man with light-colored eyes. "This is your father."

Emma tapped me on the shoulder. "Dianne, did you hear what I said?" Emma asked.

"Yes, I did," I said slowly as I reoriented myself to the present. "You said something about my father. But there's no way you know my father."

"It's because of your father, I contacted you," Emma responded.

My hands began to shake as I stared at the road in front of me. I then took a deep breath and said, "Emma, that's impossible. My father has been dead for over twenty years. He has nothing to do with this case."

"Yes, he does," Emma responded.

How?" I asked.

"He asked me to look for you."

"Emma, I don't believe you," I cried.

"Your father Louis and I were best friends at San Jose State. We used to hang out with your mother Catherine. Your father was a social science professor and your mother was a student. After your mother got pregnant, your parents moved in together. When you were a baby, your mother took off with you without telling Louis that she was leaving."

I continued to stare at the highway in front of me. "My mother told me that he had left us and didn't want to have anything to do with us."

"That's not true," Emma said. "Your father loved you."

I fought the tears welling up in my eyes. "I don't believe you. If he did, he would have come looking for me."

"He tried. Louis called your mother's parents and they refused to tell him anything. When you were ten or eleven, your father found out you and your mother were living in a homeless shelter in Los Angeles. He drove all night. When he got there, you were gone. He begged for information about you, but no one would help him."

"He should have tried more than once," I responded.

"Your father tried for years and each time the leads would go nowhere," Emma said.

"He should have tried harder. I was his child," I said.

"Dianne, your father was a fighter and he did his best. Before he died, he asked me to look for you. After he died, I tried looking on my own but I couldn't find you. Then my neighbor told me about you. It had been years since your father had died. I had no idea if you even knew about him. So I didn't know how to approach you. So I did nothing. It wasn't until I needed help with my lottery ticket, I decided to contact you."

"So you hired me based on your past relationship with my father," I said.

"I hired you, because your father did what it took to get the job done. I knew if you were his daughter, you would do the same," Emma said.

"Okay," I responded.

"Don't let me down," Emma said.

I said nothing and continued to drive. I wanted to ask Emma so many questions but I was too afraid to ask anything. Emma might give me answers that would hurt me. With $125,000 at stake, I needed to focus on the case instead of my past.

For the rest the trip, I drove in silence while my father's picture repeatedly flashed in my head.

Chapter Twenty-three

Emma and I had been waiting in line at the Secretary of State's office for twenty minutes before a middle-aged woman with a bad perm and a crooked smile greeted us.

"We need a copy of the campaign report for the recall of Judge Emma Watkins in Santa Clara County," I said.

"When was the election?" the clerk asked.

"1986," Emma said.

"1986?" The clerk gasped. "That was over twenty years ago."

"We know that," Emma snapped. "Do you have the report?"

"I'm sure it's archived. It will take some time to find it." The clerk waved a card. "You need to complete this."

I took the card. I filled it out and handed it back to the clerk.

The clerk handed us a number. "You two can sit down. I will call you when it is ready."

"Okay," I mumbled.

Emma and I sat down in silence. My head was throbbing and my lower pelvis was churning with cramps. This damn period was getting to me. I wanted to lie down, but I couldn't.

I needed chocolate. It would soothe my pain. I looked for a candy machine in the lobby and there was none. I stood up and said, "Emma, I'll be back in a few minutes."

"Where are you going?"

"I need to get chocolate."

"Why?"

"For my period."

"Chocolate is bad for the skin and it will make you even fatter," Emma snarled. "Try meditating."

I ignored Emma's comment and handed her our number. "See you in five minutes."

I left the lobby and walked down the hallway until I saw a sign for the cafeteria. I eagerly followed the sign as if it were going to lead me to a great treasure.

When I arrived at the cafeteria, there were a couple of people milling about. I looked for candy bars and there were none.

I approached a food service worker who was dressed in a white uniform that overwhelmed her slender body.

"Do you sell chocolate bars?" I asked.

"The governor banned the sale of junk food in state buildings," the worker responded.

"Why?" I asked.

"It is part of his plan to end obesity in the state. Californians are just too fat," the worker said.

"You obviously don't fall in that category."

"Last year, I was 250 pounds. I got weight loss surgery and lost over 120 pounds."

"Isn't that surgery expensive?" I asked.

"It didn't cost me anything. The state paid for it."

"That's great." So that's where my hard-earned taxpayer dollars were going. What a waste. "So do you know where I can get a chocolate bar?"

"The state has a mandate that workers aren't allowed to encourage the public to eat junk food."

"I have cramps. I need chocolate. Where can I get some?" I cried.

"Lady, calm down," the worker said. "We don't have candy, but we do have chocolate frozen yogurt."

24 Hour Lottery Ticket

"That's it?"

"Yup."

"I'll take the biggest cup possible."

The worker retrieved a cup of frozen yogurt and handed it to me. I thanked the worker and paid the cashier with my good credit card.

I sat down at an empty table and wolfed down the yogurt as if I hadn't eaten for days.

Within a few minutes, I felt my headache subsiding and my cramps lessening. I threw away the yogurt container and walked quickly back to the lobby.

I sat down next to Emma. "Did they call out our number?"

"Nope. How was your chocolate fix?"

"I had frozen chocolate yogurt," I smiled.

"Frozen yogurt? That's just fake ice cream. It's worse than candy."

I was tired of Emma's opinions. I wanted to argue with her, but instead I said nothing.

"122," the clerk called out.

"That's our number," I said.

Emma and I walked up together and handed her the number.

"We don't have the report. It was destroyed in a fire."

Emma's eyes widened. "When?"

"April 9, 1987."

"Oh my God, that was only a few months after the recall," Emma shrieked.

"What was the cause of the fire?" I asked.

"We don't have that information," the clerk responded. "You'll need to ask the city."

"Can we get a statement from you with a state seal that the report was destroyed?" I asked.

"Sure," the clerk answered. "We have a form for missing and destroyed reports."

The clerk completed the form and added the state's seal. She handed it to me.

"Thank you," I said as I put the form in my briefcase. "Do you have the address of City Hall and how to get there?"

The clerk handed me the address and gave me directions. Emma and I then walked out of the office."

"I told you that they were after me," Emma exclaimed.

"Emma, we need to find out what happened. It could have been an accident."

"I bet you believe in the tooth fairy."

"What do you mean by that?"

"You never want to see the truth when it's staring at you in the face."

24 Hour Lottery Ticket

I wanted to tell Emma to go to hell. Instead, I said, "Let's get going."

Emma and I got into our car in silence. I turned on the ignition. We then headed to City Hall.

Chapter Twenty-four

After Emma and I arrived at City Hall, we were directed to the Fire Department for the report. Sitting at the counter was a young clerk with greasy black hair and a bad complexion.

"Miss, we would like a copy of a report for a fire that occurred on April 9, 1987," I said.

"1987? That's really old. It's a year older than I am," the clerk said.

"We need the report as soon as possible," I said.

"It will take at least a week," the clerk responded.

"Why so long?" I asked.

"We don't keep the archived reports," the clerk replied, "They're in storage."

"Where?" I asked.

"I don't know," she replied.

"Miss, I would like to speak to your supervisor," I said.

"Why?" she asked.

"We need the report now," I replied. "We can't wait."

The clerk punched in a number and spoke in a low tone. Within a minute, a slender woman with a bad hair cut in her early fifties greeted us.

"What can I do for you ladies?" the woman asked.

"Ma'am, we need a report from an incident in 1987 as soon as possible," I said.

"Why?" she asked.

"I'm an attorney and we need it for court this afternoon," I responded.

"I'm sorry but we won't be able to obtain the report for you today," the woman said.

"We need the report now," Emma interjected.

"The report is in storage," the woman replied.

"Can't you give us the address so we can pick it up?" I asked.

"It's not that simple. We have a process," the woman responded.

"Ma'am, this report will make an enormous difference in my client's life," I said.

"What's your case about?" the woman asked.

"I can't tell you," I responded. "It's attorney-client privilege."

The woman glared at us. "Ladies, you come here at the last minute to retrieve a twenty year old report. You won't tell me what your case is about. My hands are tied."

Emma's face became contorted and red. "Lady, it's really none of your business why we need the report. You have a duty to give it to us now."

"I couldn't even if I wanted to," the woman responded. "It's not in Sacramento."

"Where is it?" Emma asked.

"In Redding," she replied.

"Why there?" Emma asked.

"A private company in Redding warehouses all our old reports," the woman said. "It's a lot cheaper than keeping them here."

"Wasting taxpayer dollars on corporations is an insult to city workers," Emma snarled.

"It's done all the time," the woman replied.

"How far is Redding?" I asked.

"It's at least a two hour drive," the woman responded.

Two hours? There was no way we could go there and get back in time for court.

24 Hour Lottery Ticket

"Ma'am, do you remember a fire back in 1987 at the Secretary of State's building?" I asked.

The supervisor stared down at the counter and mumbled, "I wasn't working for the department back then."

"Is there anyone who we can talk to?" I asked.

"No," the supervisor mumbled again.

"Who was the Fire Chief in 1987?" I asked.

"I don't know," she responded.

"Can you look him up?" Emma asked.

The woman punched in a few codes on the computer.

"Donald Copper," the woman said.

"Where is he now?" Emma asked.

"Dead," the woman replied. "He died back in 2004."

"Ma'am is there another way we can find out the cause of the fire?" I asked.

"The local paper has archives that go back to 1980," the woman responded.

"Can you look up the articles for us?" I asked.

"No I can't," the woman responded. "We don't have access to the Internet."

"Why not?" I asked.

"Too many workers were surfing the Internet," she said. "The City Manager turned it off. The only place you can get it is at the library."

"Can you give us the address and directions?" I asked.

The supervisor wrote down the address along with directions. She then handed me a piece of paper.

We bid the supervisor goodbye and exited the building. We got into our car.

"She is such a liar," Emma snapped.

"What are you talking about?" I said.

"She knows what happened," Emma responded.

"How do you know that?" I asked.

"Because she wouldn't look at us when we asked her if she knew anything about the fire," Emma said. "She wouldn't refer us to anyone."

"Why didn't you say something?" I asked.

"It was pointless," Emma replied. "She's afraid of them."

"Emma, you're being paranoid," I said.

"No, I'm not," she snapped.

"We'll be at the library in a few minutes," I said. "After that, we'll have the answer."

"I hope you're right," Emma said.

24 Hour Lottery Ticket

Chapter Twenty-five

The library was almost empty and we easily found a computer terminal. I logged in and searched for archives of the city's newspaper. I typed in "fire," "secretary of state" and "1987." Several articles appeared.

I quickly read the articles. The first two had no real information about the cause of the fire. The third stated the following.

Secretary of State Office Gutted by Four-Alarm Fire

Sacramento Telenews

By Alan Steele, Staff Writer

April 12, 1987

Three days ago, a four-alarm fire gutted the third floor of the Secretary of State's office. Four years of campaign reports along with other election records were destroyed.

"We are devastated by the loss," said Claudia Robbins, Secretary of State. "On Monday, we will send a letter requesting political campaigns from 1982 to 1986 to voluntarily send copies of their campaign reports. They will have ninety days to respond."

Fire officials suspect that an arsonist caused the fire.

"We discovered matchbooks near the burned file cabinets," said Mark Witherspoon, Chief Investigator for the Sacramento Fire Department. "It appears that the fire was intentionally set."

The Sacramento Police Department has launched a separate investigation.

"We have taken the matchbooks into evidence," said Donald Townsend, Sergeant for Special Investigations "Unfortunately, our lab found no fingerprints."

Townsend noted that there were no witnesses to the fire and the police have no suspects.

Longtime community activist Bryce Allen believes that the arson was politically motivated.

"Politics is a dirty game. I know of at least two campaigns where the contributions came from dirty sources and the treasurers were clean as sewer water. I bet they burned up the reports to cover up their tracks," said Allen.

When asked to name the campaigns, Allen refused to answer.

Fire and police officials will continue their investigation.

The public is asked if they have information about the fire to contact the Fire Department's hotline at (916) 555-FIRE.

Emma and I glanced at the remaining of the articles. The last one gave the status of the investigation.

No Suspects Linked to Secretary of State Fire

Sacramento Telenews

Alan Steele, Staff Writer

July 25, 1987

After three months of investigation, fire and police officials have been unable to identify a suspect for the fire that destroyed records in the Secretary of State's office.

"We have followed up diligently on all tips," said Fire Chief Rueben Trimble. "Unfortunately, they have been unfruitful."

Last Friday, the deadline passed for campaigns from 1982 to 1986 to voluntarily resubmit reports. As of yesterday, less than 10 percent of the campaigns had complied with the request.

"We are very disappointed with the lack of response. We hope to pass legislation that will mandate the destroyed reports are re-filed with our office," said Secretary of State Claudia Robbins.

Assemblymember Gerry Rynette (R-San Diego) is the sponsor of the bill. The bill has garnered some support from both parties. However, the Governor who is a political opponent of the Secretary of State has vowed to veto it.

"The Secretary of State was negligent because she failed to warehouse the reports in a fireproof safe. Campaigns should not be penalized for her negligence," said Governor Gerard Bloome.

There were no other articles about the case. I printed the articles and handed them to Emma.

I turned to Emma and said, "You're right, it was arson."

"Told you."

"But we still don't have enough to show that the arson was linked to your campaign," I said.

"Yes, we do," Emma countered.

"No, we don't," I responded. "We have no idea why the fire was set and the person who did it was never caught. We're at a dead end."

"Dianne, you are missing an important fact."

"What?" I asked.

"The woman at the Fire Department lied to us about the name of the Fire Chief," Emma responded.

"What do you mean?" I asked.

"She said his name was Donald Copper and he was dead. And the newspaper said it was Rueben Trimble," Emma replied.

"Perhaps, she punched in the wrong code in the computer."

"I don't think so," Emma said. "She deliberately tried to mislead us."

"It doesn't really matter who the fire chief was, because they never found the culprit."

"But she knows," Emma said.

"That's ridiculous," I said. "She wasn't even working at the Fire Department back then."

"We need to go back to her and find out the truth," Emma responded.

"Fine," I said.

We left the library and headed back to the Fire Department.

Chapter Twenty-six

Emma and I took the elevator to the Fire Department. When we were about to exit, Emma turned to me and said, "I have to go to the bathroom."

"Again?" I said.

"What do you mean? It's been a while."

"An hour is not a long time. You really need to get your bladder checked."

"You should mind your own business," Emma snapped.

I wanted to lash out at Emma for her rudeness. Instead I said, "I'll see you in a few minutes."

We exited the elevator. Emma walked to the bathroom. While I was waiting for Emma, I heard a beep from my cell phone. I had a text message. It read: *Old bitch, stay away from Shawn. He's all mine, Amber.*

I walked a few yards in the opposite direction of the women's bathroom. I then hit the button to call Shawn's number. After a few seconds, Shawn picked up.

"Baby, what's up?"

"Shawn, who the hell is Amber?"

"Jesus Christ, she hacked into my e-mail again."

"Who is she?"

"Nobody, baby."

"Don't bullshit me."

"Calm down, Dianne," Shawn replied. "Before we got back together, I went out with Amber a few times. Nothing serious and it's over."

"Then why is she sending rude text messages?" I asked.

"Amber is really possessive. She's young and doesn't have a lot of self confidence," Shawn responded.

"And she doesn't understand your relationship is over."

"It's kind of complicated," Shawn said.

"How?" I asked.

"Amber caused the break-up of my marriage. She text messaged Lauren about us. After Lauren found out, she demanded that I move out."

"I still don't understand why Amber thinks you two are a couple."

"Because I'm temporarily staying with her."

I felt my blood pressure rising. "Why?" I shouted.

"I didn't have a choice. I didn't want to lose my house. You know when Lauren and I bought our home, we got a really good rate. That rate is over. A couple months ago, our mortgage doubled. I couldn't afford to pay rent and the mortgage, too. So I moved in with Amber."

"How old is Amber?" I asked.

"She's kind of young," Shawn replied.

"Shawn, answer my question. How old is she?"

"She'll be 22 next week."

"Chasing after children is pathetic. You're almost 40 years old. You're old enough to be her father."

"Dianne, I told you nothing is going on between us anymore."

"For God's sake, you could rent a room somewhere."

"I'm too old for that."

"But not too old to stay with a 21 year old girl you screwed and probably are still screwing."

"What was I supposed to do? Lose the house?"

"You know there's more to life than owning a house."

"I would expect an answer like that from you. Your credit is shot to hell. You've lost your apartment. If you didn't have your office, you'd be homeless."

"Go to hell," I yelled.

"That's real mature, Dianne. Unlike you, I care about my credit."

"Whatever," I said.

"You know you're just like your mother."

"What does that mean?" I snapped. "I'm not a drunk. I don't even drink."

"How many times did you and your mother end up in shelters because she couldn't hold a job? You and your mother were always being evicted. Your mother never understood how to manage money and you don't either."

"At least, my mother took care of me unlike your parents who abandoned you."

"I had foster parents who cared about me. You never even met your father and your mother was never a real mother."

"God, you're an asshole."

"Dianne, calling me names is not going to change anything. You need to get a grip on life and end this bullshit practice of being an attorney. Go back to the county and ask for your old job before you end up homeless."

"My old job doesn't exist. The county cut the position a few months ago because of the budget crisis."

"Then find a real job that pays money or you'll end up on the streets."

"Shawn, I am sick of you and your insults. And I'm sick of the lies. Just stay away from me."

"You'll come back to me," Shawn smirked. "You always do."

"Not this time, it's over. Tell your little girlfriend, you're all hers. Don't call me, e-mail or text me," I said as I hit the end button.

After a few seconds, I heard my phone buzzing. I saw Shawn's phone number. I turned off my phone and stuffed it in my purse.

I felt a tap on my shoulder. I turned around. It was Emma.

"Are you okay?"

"Yeah," I lied.

"Who were you talking to?" Emma asked.

"Nobody important."

"Love always causes problems," she said while touching my arm.

I decided to ignore Emma's comment. I didn't want her to know my business. "Emma, we're on deadline," I said. "We need to focus on the case."

"I'm feeling a little tired," Emma yawned. "I'll join you in a couple of minutes."

"Sure."

24 Hour Lottery Ticket

I left Emma in the hallway. I walked into the lobby and approached the reception desk. The same young clerk was behind it.

"I'd like to see your supervisor again."

"What for?" the girl asked.

"I just need to see her."

"She's real busy."

"Miss, I don't have time for games. My client needs information from her."

"The old lady?" the girl asked.

"The politically correct term is senior citizen," I said.

"Whatever," the girl sneered. "She's old as my grandma."

"Anyway, I want you to call your supervisor now. If you don't, I will file a complaint against you."

"You wouldn't do that."

"The complaint will be filed in the next hour and your job will be gone tomorrow."

"Give me a break. People have complained before and nothing happened."

"Miss, my client's life depends on speaking to your supervisor."

"Why? Does she have cancer?" she asked.

I paused for a few seconds. From the corner of my eye, I saw Emma walking toward us.

"No, she doesn't," I replied.

"Then what? She's too old for AIDS."

Emma's voice boomed, "Of course not, I always practice safe sex."

I was taken aback by Emma's comment. With her messy apartment and rude demeanor, I couldn't imagine her being with anyone.

"You're too old to have sex," the clerk said.

Emma's face turned red. "Young lady, once you learn how to make another person pleasure you the way you like it, you'll never want to stop no matter how old you are. People need sex like they need food and water. It's an essential."

The clerk's eyes widened and she cracked a slight smile. "Wow, wait until I tell my grandma."

"So please buzz your supervisor," I said in a firm voice.

"Okay."

The clerk punched in the supervisor's phone number and asked her to see us. We waited for a few minutes until the supervisor appeared.

"I see you're back," the supervisor said.

"Can we take a walk down the hall?" I asked.

"Why?"

"We have a few questions," I replied.

"Ask them here."

"They're personal," I said as I looked at her directly in the eyes.

The supervisor's face did not flinch. "What do you mean by that?"

Emma interjected, "Why did you give us the wrong name for the Fire Chief?"

"What are you talking about?" she protested.

"His name was Rueben Trimble and you said his name was Donald Copper," Emma said.

"I must have punched in the wrong code by accident," the supervisor answered.

I glared at her and firmly said, "Let's take a walk down the hall."

"Okay."

We walked out of the lobby in silence. After we exited, Emma said, "So you know who caused the fire."

"No, I don't," she responded.

"Then why did you lie about the fire chief?" I asked.

"Because. . . " she faltered.

"Because what?" Emma asked.

The supervisor stared at the floor and glanced up. "Years ago, I was a young woman in a bad marriage with two kids. After I met him, things changed."

"Who?" I asked.

"Rueben," she responded.

"Did you have an affair with him?" Emma asked.

"No, I didn't," she answered.

"Then why did you lie?" I asked.

"I just didn't want anything to hurt him. He was a good man. He helped me out during my divorce. My husband was abusive. He used to beat my kids and me. When Rueben found out, he told me to leave my husband. He gave me money to move and he protected me from my husband. He was like an older brother to me."

"So I still don't understand why you lied," I said.

"Rueben helped me when I needed it. If he's in trouble for something now, it's my duty to protect him," she answered.

"Do you think he was involved in setting the fire?" I asked.

"No," she replied.

"Do you know who did it?" I asked.

"No," she answered.

"If you find out anything, please call me," I said as I handed her my card.

"I will."

"Thank you for your time," Emma said as she extended her hand. Emma and the supervisor shook hands. We then said our goodbyes.

Sacramento had been a waste of time. I was sick of this case, Shawn and everything else. However, I knew this was not the time to complain.

I turned to Emma in a calm manner and said, "Let's head back to San Jose."

Emma nodded her head.

Chapter Twenty-seven

Emma and I traveled for a couple miles until I pulled in front of Vanessa's Burgers and Shakes.

"Let's go in and get some food," I said.

"I'm fasting," she responded.

"Fasting? Is it for religious reasons?" I asked.

"Hell no, religion is for fools who need to believe in a mythical higher power. I just need to lose a pound or two. My suit is a size 4 and it's a bit tight."

Size 4? The last time I was a size 4 was probably when I was 4 years old. "Then I'll just get something for me."

"You're too damn chubby and it wouldn't hurt you to fast. Maybe if you did it for about five or six weeks, you'd be a decent size."

24 Hour Lottery Ticket

I glared at Emma. "I'm hungry and I can't concentrate. I have cramps and I need to eat."

"Then order a salad and a diet drink," Emma said. "That will help you to lose some weight."

I ignored Emma and got out of the car. I walked into the restaurant. I went up to the counter and ordered a double cheeseburger with large onion rings and an extra large chocolate milk shake. I sat down at a table next to the window by the car. I devoured my meal within a few minutes. I rubbed my belly. I felt good. Now, I was ready to deal with Emma and the case.

I walked back to the car and got into it.

"God, you're a pig," Emma scoffed. "If you keep eating that way, you'll be huge as a house."

"That's your opinion," I said.

"If your father were alive, he'd be upset," Emma sneered. "He always kept himself in shape and he had great genes. It's too bad that you didn't inherit them."

"How old was my father when he died?" I asked.

"45," Emma answered.

"Was it cancer?" I asked.

"Yes, your father died from testicular cancer."

"It must have been hard for his parents to lose him."

"They hated your father."

"Why?"

"Your father always struggled with his sexuality for much of his life. It wasn't until his late thirties that he finally found himself. When he came out to his family, they told your father that he would die in hell. When he was 44 years old, your father was diagnosed with cancer. Your father hoped that his family would help him in his time of need. To his disappointment, they told him that God was punishing him for his sins. They refused to take care of him. One year later, your father was dead."

Tears came down my face. "How could they not help their own son?" I asked.

"We can't change what your grandparents did to your father," Emma responded. "They were from another era where homophobia was accepted."

I said nothing and turned on the ignition. I was incensed by my grandparents' callousness. However, I knew that I had to get back to focusing on this case. I drove for a few blocks until I parked the car in front of a state building.

Emma's face winced as she tugged at my arm. "Why are we stopping?"

"Just follow me," I ordered as I removed Emma's hand from my arm.

"Where are we going?" Emma asked.

"To the lottery office, it's on the fourth floor. We're turning in your ticket."

"I'm not doing that," Emma protested.

24 Hour Lottery Ticket

"You either turn in your ticket now or you have the option of mailing it after we lose your case. I don't want to risk your lottery ticket getting lost in the mail."

"And you're willing to walk away from $125,000? You must be crazy."

"Emma, my first duty is to you as my client. We don't have a case. We can't link the fire to your campaign. There's not enough evidence to show you will suffer irreparable harm if your name is released."

"I'm not a quitter. We'll prevail."

"You're fooling yourself. And so what if you get bad publicity, $73 million is worth it."

"I'd rather be homeless than let people know I've won."

"Emma, you're not thinking rationally."

"Yes, I am. I didn't hire you to give up. We will fight this until the end."

"Emma, there's no point going back to the court. My friend Robyn can help with the publicity. That's her field. She can put a spin on it that will make you look good."

Emma's eyes narrowed. "So this is about your friend earning a few extra dollars from me. That's not going to happen."

"No, it's not. It's about saving your name and winning at the same time."

"Dianne, there's still time to get more evidence."

"We have to be back in court in two hours."

"What about your cell phone?"

"What about it?"

"I can make calls."

"To who?"

"People we haven't talked with."

"And what if we can't get a hold of them?"

"Dianne, sometimes trying is more important than winning."

"And you're willing to risk a $73 million lottery ticket," I said.

"Yes," Emma responded.

Chapter Twenty-eight

Emma touched my shoulder and said, "Give me your cell phone. I need to make calls."

I handed Emma my cell phone. "Who are you calling?"

"Our friend at the Fire Department, she should have the phone number for the former Fire Chief."

Emma dialed the phone number for the supervisor. She exchanged a few words with the person who picked up the phone. After a couple of minutes, Emma ended the call.

"She's gone for the day. They wouldn't give me her cell phone number."

Emma called 411. To her disappointment, there was no listing for Rueben Trimble in Sacramento.

"Do you have Internet access?"

"I use my cell phone to check my e-mail. I know there's a button that will allow me to do other things on the Internet, but I don't know how to use it."

"I can figure it out."

"I doubt it. It's too hard," I responded.

"Dianne, I know how to get on the Internet from a cell phone. I've done it before."

"Really?" I asked.

"Yes," Emma responded.

"What do you go on the Internet for?"

"Online dating. I found my last man on the Internet."

"I didn't know there were a lot of older men on the Internet."

"I'm not interested in men my age. They're flabby, boring as hell and suffer from ED."

"What's ED?"

"Erectile dysfunction," Emma sneered. "They can't get it up. That's why I only go after younger men."

I almost choked on Emma's words. I couldn't believe she was still chasing younger guys after her affair with her law clerk. But I guess some people never change.

Emma fiddled with my cell phone for a few minutes. She smiled. "We're on the Internet."

"Great."

"I did a search and found his phone number."

"That was quick."

"Yes."

Emma dialed the phone number and asked for Rueben Trimble. After a few seconds passed, she ended the call.

"Wrong number," she said.

"Is there more than one Rueben Trimble?"

"Apparently."

"Find any more numbers?"

"There's a Rueben Trimble in Houston and that's all the public phone numbers I could find."

"Try it and put it on speakerphone."

"Okay."

Emma dialed the number and let it ring several times.

A woman answered the phone. Her voice had a slight southern twang. "Hello," she said.

"May I speak to Rueben Trimble, the former Fire Chief?" Emma asked.

"My father?" the woman asked.

"Yes," Emma responded.

"He's busy," the woman said. "He's in the yard planting."

"It's important that I talk to him," Emma said.

"Why?" the woman asked.

"I am a former judge and it's personal," Emma said.

"Is daddy in some kind of trouble?" the woman asked.

"No," Emma responded.

"Okay, I'll go get him."

There was dead silence on the cell phone for a minute or two until Mr. Trimble picked up.

"Hello, my daughter said you wanted to talk to me. Who are you?"

"My name is Emma Watkins and I am a former judge. I'm in a car with my lawyer."

"Former? Are you retired?" Mr. Trimble asked.

"No. I was recalled back in 1986," Emma responded.

"That was a long time ago," Mr. Trimble said.

"Do you remember the fire that destroyed campaign reports in 1987?" Emma asked.

"Yes," Mr. Trimble responded.

"Do you know who did it?" Emma asked.

"We never found the culprits, but we had a couple of suspects," Mr. Trimble answered.

"Who?" I asked.

"They were from out of town. But the police wouldn't cooperate."

"What police?" Emma asked.

"San Jose," Mr. Trimble answered.

I almost let out a squeal, but I restrained myself.

"Did they tell you why?" Emma asked.

"They felt there wasn't enough evidence to connect the fire to the suspects," Mr. Trimble answered.

"And you believed them," Emma said.

"My gut feeling was the cops had been paid off. But I couldn't prove anything."

"Who were the suspects?'" I asked.

"I don't remember," Mr. Trimble replied.

"We need this information ASAP," Emma said.

"I don't have it," Mr. Trimble said. "I don't even know if the files still exist."

"Is there anyone we can call?"

"The investigator. He's still around."

"What's his name and phone number?

Mr. Trimble dictated the information and Emma wrote it down.

I chimed in, "Mr. Trimble, are you willing to send me an e-mail about what you said?"

"Definitely," Mr. Trimble responded.

I gave him my e-mail address and said, "I need your statement for a case and we have to be back in court in two hours."

"What's the case about?"

"I can't discuss that, but please e-mail us your statement."

I told Mr. Trimble what his e-mail should include.

"I'll send it now."

"Great."

After we said our goodbyes, Emma hit the end button.

Chapter Twenty-nine

Emma dialed the phone number and hit the speakerphone button. The phone rang several times before someone picked up.

"May I speak to James Parker?"

"Parker speaking," the voice answered.

"My name is Emma Watkins and I am a former judge. My lawyer is with me. I have a few questions about a fire."

"Fire? Can you tell me the date and time of it?" Mr. Parker asked.

"April 9, 1987," Emma said. "I don't have the time."

"Jesus Christ, that was over twenty years ago," Mr. Parker said. "Our database doesn't go that far."

Emma's face bristled a bit. "I know that. Do you remember the fire at the Secretary of State's office?"

There was dead silence on the phone for a few seconds. Mr. Parker then spoke. "Yeah, I remember it. Too well in fact."

"Why?" Emma asked.

"It was one of the biggest cases I ever investigated. I spent months investigating it. In the end, no one was charged."

"Why?" Emma asked.

"We had a lousy witness," Mr. Parker responded.

"Who was the witness?" Emma asked.

"A janitor," Mr. Parker replied.

"Did he see anything?" Emma asked.

"He saw a couple guys setting the fire, but he could never ID them," Mr. Parker replied.

"Too dark at night?" Emma asked.

"No, nothing like that," Mr. Parker replied.

"Then what?" Emma asked.

"He saw them, but he suffered from a condition called face blindness," Mr. Parker answered.

"Face blindness? What's that?" Emma asked.

"People with face blindness have a very hard time remembering what people's faces look like," Mr. Parker answered. "Some can remember family members' faces, because they see them a lot. And maybe friends if they have known them for a while. But forget about strangers. The face is a virtual blob. Everybody looks the same."

"Didn't you have other evidence?" Emma asked.

"Yeah, there were matchbooks, but no fingerprints," Mr. Parker replied. "The culprits wore gloves, but we never found them."

"Anything else?" Emma asked.

"Yeah, some hair fragments. We did some forensic testing and we came up with a couple of names."

Emma's eyes widened. "Do you remember their names?"

"I sure do," he said. "William Eggrose and Barry Bickaree."

"Can you tell me what you remember about them?" Emma asked.

"They were from San Jose. One was a small time petty thief whose father managed to keep him out of jail. He later changed his ways and went on to San Jose State University.

"The other had a couple small things like being picked up for possession of marijuana and drinking in public, but he was never convicted."

"How old were they when the fire happened?"

"Early or mid-twenties. I really don't remember. It's been a while," Mr. Parker said.

"Why would two San Jose kids set a fire in Sacramento?" Emma asked.

"Both their fathers were heavily involved in politics in San Jose. One was the biggest contributor in the Mayor's race. He must have given him over a hundred grand. He controlled the Mayor like a puppet.

"The other owned a bunch of real estate and he was San Jose's biggest developer. Some say that he used to give the Mayor a plain brown paper bag stuffed with money so he could get his contracts."

"I still don't understand the connection to the Secretary of State's fire," I said.

"They wanted the campaign reports destroyed," Mr. Parker responded.

"Why?" Emma asked.

"They were under investigation for laundering drug money through political campaigns. Back then, there were no campaign contribution limits. They would give the campaign money and the campaign would cut a check for a phony expense. Over twenty million dollars had been laundered through dozens of campaigns over a four year period."

"Were they ever charged?" I asked.

"Nope. After the reports were destroyed in Sacramento, the State didn't have anything."

"But what about the hair fragments, wouldn't that be enough to charge the sons?" Emma asked.

24 Hour Lottery Ticket

"The evidence was stolen and the lab reports were destroyed," Mr. Parker replied. "So we were left with nothing."

"Couldn't you reconstruct the case?"

"We tried, but the DA wouldn't touch the case. And the San Jose police wouldn't help us either."

"What about the copies of the campaign reports in San Jose?" Emma asked.

"Most of them got lost and others were damaged."

"How were the reports damaged?" Emma asked.

"I don't remember the details," Mr. Parker responded.

"Do you remember the names of the campaigns?" Emma asked.

"No, it would take a few days or more to get that information," Mr. Parker responded.

"Does the campaign supporting the recall of Judge Emma Watkins sound familiar?" Emma asked.

"Sorry judge, I don't remember the specific names," Mr. Parker answered.

"Is it possible?" Emma asked.

"Maybe. I need to see the reports."

"That will be too late. We need to be in court in the next hour or so."

"What for?" Mr. Parker asked.

"Can't discuss it."

"Judge, I wish you the best with your case."

I said, "Mr. Parker, before you go, I need you to send an e-mail stating what you told us."

"When do you need it?" Mr. Parker asked.

"'Right now," I responded.

"I'll do it now," Mr. Parker replied.

I rattled off my e-mail address and told Mr. Parker what his statement needed to include.

"Thanks for talking to us," I said.

"Sure," Mr. Parker responded.

Emma hit the end button and put down the phone. I glanced at my watch. With no traffic, we would make it back to court in time.

Chapter Thirty

Emma fiddled with the phone for a minute or two. She exclaimed, "I finally found him."

"Who?" I asked.

"My ex-law clerk." Emma smiled.

"The guy you had an affair with," I said.

"Yeah," Emma replied.

"I don't think we should call him," I said.

"He might be able to tell us some things," Emma countered.

"Like what?" I asked.

"Look, if we don't ask, we won't know," Emma responded.

"Okay," I said.

Emma punched in his number like an excited schoolgirl and hit the speakerphone button.

The phone rang a few times before a man answered. "Hello, this is Brad Culver speaking."

"Brad, it's Emma Watkins."

The phone was silent for a few seconds. Brad then spoke. "Emma, why are you calling me?"

"I need your help," Emma responded.

"What's that noise? Do you have me on speakerphone?" Brad asked.

"Yes," Emma responded.

"Turn it off," Brad demanded.

"My lawyer is the only one here and she knows everything."

The phone was silent again. "Emma, it's been years since we've talked. There's nothing I can do for you," Brad said angrily.

"It's important. It's for a major case," Emma pleaded.

"What is it?" Brad asked.

Emma faltered. "I don't know if I should tell you."

I chimed in, "Brad, my name is Dianne Canton and I'm Emma's attorney. We can't discuss Emma's case because of attorney-client privilege."

Brad cleared his throat. "For God's sake, we're all attorneys. I need to know the details. Emma, just tell me."

"I can't," Emma answered.

"Then you're wasting my time," Brad said.

Emma took a deep breath and gave Brad a synopsis of her case.

The phone was silent again.

"So you're doing this to avoid publicity," Brad said.

"Exactly," Emma answered.

"God knows I thought my career was ruined when the media came out about our affair. I was a new lawyer starting out. I thought I would never work again. I had to rebuild my life," Brad said.

"After the recall, I had nothing to do with law," Emma said.

"I didn't have that option. I had student loans so I needed to practice law. I left San Jose and moved to Tulare County to put it behind me," Brad said.

"So things have worked out," Emma said.

"Yes, I'm married with a teenage daughter. My wife and I are active in the church. And my wife volunteers a lot of time with the Republican Party."

"Does your wife know about us?" Emma asked.

"No, she doesn't," Brad answered. "No one does here. It's a closed chapter of my life."

"I figured that. That's why I didn't want publicity."

"So you're protecting me?"

"Brad, I followed your career. You've done well in the District Attorney's office. Most would think you're on track to be the next District Attorney in Tulare County."

"But you know that's not possible," Brad said.

"Yes, I know," Emma responded.

"So what do you want from me?" Brad asked.

"I need you to run background checks on Barry Bickaree and William Eggrose," Emma said.

"Why?" Brad asked.

"They're the ones who were involved in setting the fire, but they were never charged."

"Emma, I can't use county property to do the background checks," Brad protested. "I could lose my job."

"Then go someplace where you can," Emma ordered.

"When do you need it?" Brad asked.

"In 45 minutes," Emma said.

"Emma, I need more time," Brad responded.

"Sorry, that's all I have. We're due back in court then," Emma said.

"Can't you ask the judge for more time?" Brad asked.

"She's a major bitch and won't give us any more time," Emma responded.

"Who's the judge?" Brad asked.

"Lynda Belkin," Emma replied.

"Oh shit, I know her," Brad said.

"How?" Emma asked.

"I used to date her niece Janet," Brad replied.

"You're kidding," Emma shrieked. "Did Lynda know about you two?"

"Yeah, we dated back in college and through first year of law school. We broke up after Janet went through a personal crisis," Brad responded.

"What was it?" Emma asked.

"Emma, I don't know if I should tell you," Brad said.

"Dammit Brad, just tell me," Emma demanded.

"Janet went 5150 and had a nervous breakdown. She just couldn't handle the stress of law school. She dropped out and then gave up on life. Since then, Janet has been in and out of psych wards."

"Brad, are you willing to issue a statement?" Emma asked.

"I don't know," Brad answered.

"Brad, we need to recuse Lynda and get her off the case," Emma responded.

"I'll write something up. Where do I send it?" Brad asked.

"E-mail it to my lawyer." Emma then told Brad my e-mail address.

"Anything else?" Brad asked.

"No, just call me when you get that information," Emma said.

"No problem," Brad answered.

Emma hit the end button and put the phone down. I stared at the freeway. We just had made it to San Leandro. Thirty more minutes and we would be in San Jose.

Chapter Thirty-one

Emma handed me my cell phone and said, "It's for you."

"Dianne speaking," I answered.

"Dianne, it's Shawn."

"I can't talk to you now," I stammered. "I'm driving with a client."

"Dianne, I'm leaving Amber. Next week, I'm moving into a room."

A room? My brain told me Shawn was lying, but my heart wanted to believe him.

"Shawn, I really have to go," I said. "I will call you later." I fiddled with the phone and tried to hit the end button.

To my dismay, Shawn's voice boomed from the speakerphone. "Dianne, you and I belong together. I want you more than anything else. I don't want my wife

Lauren, and I don't want Amber. You're the only one for me."

My face turned red. Jesus Christ, I had hit the wrong button. "Shawn, I'm hanging up now," I said. I then hit the end button and put the cell phone down.

Emma grabbed the cell phone and touched my shoulder. "A man who has a wife and a girlfriend doesn't love you. Take it from someone who has played around. A person who cheats with you will cheat on you."

I stared at Emma for a few seconds and said nothing.

Emma touched me again and said, "Stay away from him."

I decided not to respond. Emma put her hand on my shoulder and said, "You're going back to him, why?"

I turned to Emma and said, "I don't want to talk about it."

"You need to," Emma responded. "Your father would be disappointed."

"Emma, don't bring my father into this. I never even met the man and he's dead."

"It doesn't matter. His spirit still lives."

"So I guess my father had problems with your affair," I said.

"No, my situation was different. I was in a loveless marriage and I never wanted to hurt anyone," Emma responded.

"Neither did I," I responded.

24 Hour Lottery Ticket

"You deserve better and I don't understand why you were involved with this married guy. Did he give you money?" Emma asked.

"No," I responded.

"You slept with a married man and he gave you nothing," Emma sneered. "How pathetic."

"I'm not a prostitute. I've never been with a man for that reason."

"You were stupid for giving it up for nothing," Emma responded.

"Emma, I don't want to talk about this anymore," I said.

"He must be really good in bed. I bet he knows how to eat..."

"Emma," I interrupted. "That's enough." I then turned up the radio loud to listen to the news for a few minutes. There were the usual stories about the latest killings in the Bay Area, corporate layoffs and the recession.

"Turn it off," Emma bristled. "The news is depressing."

I nodded my head. I then moved my hand to hit the off button. Before I could touch it, a female reporter's voice boomed, "Will the winner of San Jose's $73 million lottery ticket come forward today?"

Emma and I stared at the radio in disbelief. I touched the dial to turn up the volume.

The reporter continued. "180 days ago, a lottery ticket was bought at Jenny's Liquor Store in downtown San Jose. The lottery ticket must be turned in today or the winner will not be entitled to any of the winnings. The winning numbers are 4, 9, 27, 39, 43 and 22. We interviewed people in San Jose on why they thought the lottery winner has not claimed the prize yet."

A young woman answered, "The ticket was lost."

A middle-aged man said, "It was destroyed in the washing machine."

An older woman spoke, "They're already rich and they don't need the money."

A young guy answered, "Dude, they're probably stoned out of their mind and have no idea they won."

The reporter returned. "Lottery officials have told us that the Lottery office in South San Jose is open today until 4:30. The winner can turn in the ticket to claim his or her prize. Alternatively, the lottery ticket can be mailed today. Lottery officials say that the lottery ticket must be postmarked before midnight to be valid. In San Jose, the downtown post office is open until 9:00.

"There are no other post offices that are open after 9:00 in Northern California. Lottery officials tell us that if the lottery ticket is lost in the mail, the winner will not be entitled to anything. This is Susanne Hernandez reporting live from San Jose."

I turned off the radio and glanced at my watch. It was 3:43. I turned to Emma and said, "Like I told you back in Sacramento, there is no guarantee we're going to win. We can skip court and drive to the Lottery office in

South San Jose. We can be there in about fifteen minutes."

Emma scowled, "I can't believe you're willing to walk away from your contingency fee of $125,000. There's no way in hell I'm going to run to a flock of hungry reporters."

I protested, "Emma, my top priority is you and not my contingency fee. This could be your last chance. If we lose the case, your only option will be to mail in the ticket and it could be lost."

"No, my only option will be to destroy the ticket. There is no way I will allow my name to be publicized."

"Are you sure?"

"Dianne, go to court. That's an order."

"But Emma. . ."

Emma ignored me. I looked straight ahead and said nothing. There was no point arguing with her. Emma had made her decision and as her lawyer, I was obligated to follow it.

Chapter Thirty-two

Emma and I took the elevator to Judge Belkin's courtroom. Juan was sitting in the front with a large briefcase. I motioned for Emma to sit down. I then approached the court clerk and told her that Emma and I were here for our 4:00 p.m. appointment.

The court clerk responded, "I will let Judge Belkin know that you are here."

I left the clerk's desk and walked to where Emma was seated. I sat down and pulled out my notepad from my briefcase. I scratched out a brief outline for our case. I showed it to Emma and she nodded her head.

A couple minutes later, the clerk announced, "Counsel, the honorable Judge Belkin will see you."

We followed Juan into the judge's chambers. We all sat down. Judge Belkin was seated behind her desk. The judge's round face was flushed and her frizzy hair was damp with perspiration.

"The Court ordered petitioner to obtain a certified copy of the recall campaign report from the Secretary of State's office. Ms. Canton, do you have a copy for the court's review?" asked Judge Belkin.

"Your honor, before petitioner delves into the issue of the campaign report, petitioner hereby places another request that the court recuse itself from hearing matter on the ground that. . ."

Judge Belkin's face turned red as she interrupted me. "Ms. Canton, your request for recusal was denied this morning. I warned you not to raise this issue again."

Juan interjected, "The state concurs. A ruling was already made by this court."

I cleared my throat and said, "Your honor, petitioner has new grounds. She was unaware of these new facts until this afternoon."

The judge responded, "What are petitioner's so-called new facts?"

"This afternoon, petitioner was informed that your niece Janet Belkin had a long-term relationship with Brad Culver.

Petitioner previously testified she and had an affair with Mr. Culver. Their affair was splashed on the front page of the newspaper just a week before the recall election."

"Counsel, my patience is beginning to wane. My niece's personal affairs have nothing do with this case."

Juan interjected, "The state has no interest in the past relationships of the honorable Judge Belkin's niece."

"Judge Belkin, we have a statement from Brad Culver that will show that your honor knew about your niece's relationship with him and the reason why the relationship ended."

Judge Belkin's eyes narrowed. "Counsel, what is your point? Relationships end all the time."

"Your honor, petitioner's career was destroyed by the exposure of their affair. Your niece and petitioner dated the same man. The court has a clear conflict of interest."

"Ms. Canton, there is a major difference between my niece and petitioner. My niece was a single woman. Petitioner, on the other hand, was a married woman. So the consequences were different."

"Different? Oh yes, your honor, they were different. Your niece was committed to a mental institution; whereas, petitioner became an alcoholic."

Judge Belkin's face reddened. "The court has heard enough. We will not discuss my niece further."

"We need to discuss your niece. If we don't, petitioner will have no option but to file a complaint with the Judicial Commission."

Judge Belkin scowled, "Counsel, you will not threaten me with an unjustified complaint."

"Petitioner would like a court reporter present in order that petitioner's request for recusal can be part of the court's record."

"Your request is denied," Judge Belkin responded.

"Why?" I asked.

"Counsel, it's denied. Period. Do not ask for a court reporter again. If you do, the court will hold you in contempt."

"If we cannot have a court reporter, we still need to resolve the issue of recusal," I said.

"Counsel, did my niece and petitioner date Mr. Culver at the same time?" Judge Belkin asked.

"No, they did not," I responded. "Your niece's relationship occurred prior to petitioner's."

"The court then finds that it has no conflict of interest. Their relationships with Mr. Culver were separate and distinct. Therefore, your motion for recusal is denied."

Emma nudged me and whispered, "Hand me your cell phone. I need to call Brad."

"Your honor, petitioner would like to request a three minute recess," I said. "Petitioner needs to make a phone call."

"Denied," Judge Belkin responded.

"Your honor, this call is critical to the outcome of petitioner's case."

"Denied. The call should have been made prior."

Emma folded her arms. "Your honor, with or without your permission, we will make the call."

Judge Belkin responded, "If you do, I will hold you in contempt."

I interjected, "Your honor, my client's life is on the line. We apologize for the last minute request. However, if her request is denied, she could die if her name is publicized."

Judge Belkin glared at me. "The court will grant a three minute recess. Be back at 4:25."

Chapter Thirty-three

Emma and I walked out of the courtroom into the conference room. I handed Emma my cell phone. She dialed Brad's phone number and hit the speakerphone button. On the third ring, Brad answered.

"Brad, it's Emma. Did you find anything?"

"Yeah, I did. William Eggrose was heavily involved in San Jose politics. He picked the last two mayors. A nasty political mailer came out three years ago in the last mayor's race. Eggrose was charged with violating ethical rules, but nothing came of it."

Emma's eyes widened. "How interesting. Who was the mayor's opponent back then?"

"Khanh Sanchez. She was progressive, good looking, and charismatic. She was the perfect racial mix —Vietnamese and Mexican. Sanchez and her opponent were in a dead heat race. Sanchez's husband was the head of a local multi-cultural community agency.

"A week before the election, a political mailer went out charging Sanchez's husband with sexually harassing two staffers at his agency. Sanchez tried to refute the charges, but the press didn't care. She lost the election by less than 100 votes.

"It later came out that the staffers had been paid to fabricate the charges. Eggrose was charged, but no one was ever able to show that he was behind the mailer."

"That's some real interesting stuff. What about Barry Bickaree?" Emma asked.

"Bickaree has had a bunch of dead end jobs. He has three or four kids with different mothers. He's a total loser."

"Can you e-mail my lawyer what you found about William Eggrose?" Emma asked.

"Sure," Brad answered. "When do you need it?"

"Right now. We're due back in court in thirty seconds."

"Anything else?"

"No," Emma answered. She then hit the end button and handed me my cell phone.

Chapter Thirty-four

Emma and I walked into the judge's chambers and sat down. Juan was already seated.

Judge Belkin folded her arms and looked directly at me. "Counsel, did you get a certified copy of the campaign report?"

"Your honor, petitioner and I went to the Secretary of State's office. Within a few months of the recall of petitioner, there was a fire. The campaign report was apparently destroyed."

I pulled out the statement from my briefcase and handed it to Judge Belkin. "We believe that the fire was set by petitioner's opponents."

Judge Belkin asked, "Was there anyone convicted?"

"No one was convicted."

"Was anyone charged?" Judge Belkin asked.

"No," I answered.

Juan interjected, "Petitioner's case is based on all pure conjecture. She has no case."

Emma cocked her head and glared at Juan. "Yes, we do. Any fool could see that the fire was set so no one could find out the truth."

Judge Belkin turned to Emma. "You are not to speak unless I give you permission. Do you understand?"

Emma nodded her head and mumbled, "Yes, I do."

I looked into the judge's eyes directly and said, "We believe that the sons of two San Jose political insiders were involved in setting the fire. The San Jose police refused to cooperate. So they were never charged."

Juan interrupted, "Objection, hearsay."

I responded, "Your honor, we have statements from witnesses that support petitioner's argument."

Juan said, "Objection. Your honor, the statements are still hearsay. They're out of court statements."

"Your honor, there is no time for the witnesses to travel. One lives in Texas. The others live in Sacramento and the Central Valley."

Juan responded, "Then the statements should not be allowed. Petitioner had 180 days to file an action in court. Yet, she waited until the very last day to file. She should have filed sooner."

I responded, "Your honor, it is irrelevant when petitioner filed her case. It doesn't matter whether she filed today or a month ago. The real issue is that she will be irreparably harmed if her name is released. We must keep petitioner safe from foul play."

Juan interjected, "That's all speculation. Petitioner has not provided one shred of evidence that her life is at risk."

Judge Belkin responded, "You both have presented compelling arguments. Before the court can make a ruling, we must consider the testimony of the witnesses."

Judge Belkin turned to me and asked, "Can petitioner's witnesses testify by telephone?"

I answered, "I don't know."

Juan interjected, "Your honor, this is the age of the cell phone. Surely, the witnesses must have cell phones or access to one. It is imperative that the state have the opportunity to cross-examine petitioner's witnesses. Anything short of this would not only be a mockery of justice, but also would be an insult to the people of California."

Judge Belkin responded, "I will allow petitioner a ten minute break to contact her witnesses. If the witnesses are unable to testify by telephone, the court then will make a ruling on whether to admit the statements as evidence. Be back in my chambers by 4:55 sharp."

Chapter Thirty-five

Emma turned to me in the conference room and said, "Juan is such an asshole."

"He's just doing his job."

Emma made a wry face. I ignored her and pulled out my cell phone. "Emma, let's start lining up our witnesses."

I called former Fire Chief Rueben Trimble and the investigator James Parker. They both agreed to be witnesses.

I put down my cell phone and said, "Brad is the only person left."

"Let me call him," Emma said.

Emma took my cell phone, dialed Brad's phone number, and hit the speakerphone button. The phone rang several times and Brad's voice mail came on with the message: "You have reached the desk of Chief Assistant District Attorney Brad Culver. I am away from my desk. Please leave your name, phone number, and message. If you need to get in touch with me right away, please call my cell phone at (559) 555-1245."

Emma hit the end button and dialed Brad's cell phone number. After a couple rings, Brad picked up.

"Brad, it's Emma."

"Emma, I e-mailed you the information," Brad responded.

"Thanks. I need one more thing from you," Emma said.

"What?"

"I need you to be a witness for my case. The judge agreed that you could testify by telephone."

Brad was silent for a few seconds. "Emma, I can't."

"Why not?" Emma asked.

"I won't add anything to the case."

"Brad, if I lose my case, our affair will become public. And I don't think you want your wife to find out about us."

"You were before my marriage. The past is the past."

"And she knows nothing about us. Nor do the people in your church. If you want to keep your all-American boy image, you will testify."

"Emma, are you trying to blackmail me?"

Emma purred, "Honey, of course not. I just want to help you keep your past in the past."

"Dammit Emma, I need to think about this."

"You've got five minutes."

"Five minutes isn't enough time."

"How about fifteen?" Emma asked.

"No, I need at least an hour," Brad responded.

"Too long. My case could be decided by then and the reporters will be knocking on your door."

Brad groaned. "Give me twenty minutes and I'll call you back."

"Brad, you have twenty minutes and not a second more. And you'd better come back with the right answer."

"Emma, I've got to go."

Emma hit the end button and handed me the cell phone.

"Emma, do you think he'll testify?"

Emma responded, "Brad was never the pansy type."

"What does that mean?"

"He doesn't like being controlled."

"So he won't testify."

"We'll see what happens."

I wanted to tell Emma that wasn't good enough. Instead, I glanced at my watch and said, "Emma, let's go back in."

Chapter Thirty-six

I told the judge about our witnesses and gave her their phone numbers.

"Counsel, you may proceed," Judge Belkin said.

The judge put her phone on speakerphone and dialed Rueben Trimble's phone number. After a couple of rings, he picked up.

"Mr. Trimble, it's Dianne Canton, Emma Watkins' attorney. Are you ready to testify?"

"Yes," Mr. Trimble responded.

Judge Belkin administered an oath to Mr. Trimble. She nodded her head in my direction.

"Mr. Trimble, do you remember a fire at the Secretary of State's office back in 1987?" I asked.

"Yes, I do," Mr. Trimble responded.

"Please tell us about the fire."

"I was the Fire Chief for the Sacramento Fire Department. A fire broke out in the early morning in that office. It was a four-alarm fire. Documents were destroyed and the building suffered a lot of damage."

"Were campaign reports destroyed?" I asked.

"Yes," Mr. Trimble answered.

"What years?" I asked.

"1982 to 1986," Mr. Trimble responded.

"Petitioner Emma Watkins was recalled in 1986. Was her opponents' campaign report destroyed?"

"All the campaign reports were housed in the same place. If Ms. Watkins' opponents filed their report, it would have been destroyed."

"Mr. Trimble, what was the cause of the fire?"

"Our investigation determined it was arson," Mr. Trimble responded.

"Did the suspect live in Sacramento?" I asked.

"There were two suspects and they did not live in Sacramento," Mr. Trimble replied.

"Where did they live?" I asked.

"Both of them lived in San Jose," Mr. Trimble responded.

"Were they arrested?" I asked.

"No, they were not," Mr. Trimble replied.

"Why not?" I asked.

"The San Jose police would not cooperate in our investigation," Mr. Trimble said.

"Why not?" I asked.

"Because the suspects' families were connected to some San Jose politicians, the police were totally useless," Mr. Trimble replied.

I cocked my head in Judge Belkin's direction. "I have no further questions for this witness."

Judge Belkin nodded her head. "Mr. Segura, you may proceed."

"Mr. Trimble, did you personally investigate the fire?" Juan asked.

"No, I did not," Mr. Trimble replied. "Our investigator James Parker did."

"So everything you know is based on his investigation, correct?"

"Correct," Mr. Trimble answered.

"So you never independently verified his findings, correct?" Juan asked.

"James Parker had been with the department for over fifteen years and he was the best," Mr. Trimble responded.

"Mr. Trimble, who were the suspects in the investigation?" Juan asked.

"I don't remember their names," Mr. Trimble replied.

"What do you remember about them?" Juan asked.

"They were some young punks out of San Jose," Mr. Trimble responded. "Their fathers played hard ball with the politicos."

"Were the suspects interviewed?" Juan asked.

"No, their lawyers wouldn't allow it," Mr. Trimble responded.

"And what about the San Jose police?" Juan asked.

"As I said before, they were useless," Mr. Trimble replied.

"What do you mean by that?" Juan asked.

"The police chief wouldn't return our calls," Mr. Trimble responded. "James Parker even went down and they refused to help him."

"Why would you need the San Jose police to be involved?" Juan asked.

"To help us gather evidence," Mr. Trimble responded.

"Mr. Trimble, what kind of evidence?" Juan asked.

"Interview those who knew the suspects, their friends and families. To find out the motive behind the crime," Mr. Trimble said.

"Couldn't the Sacramento police have done that?" Juan asked.

"Sacramento is 120 miles from San Jose," Mr. Trimble replied. "And we didn't have the resources to investigate."

"So a thorough investigation was never done, correct?" Juan asked.

"We did the best we could," Mr. Trimble replied.

"Isn't it possible that the suspects were innocent of the crime, correct?" Juan asked.

I said, "Objection, calls for speculation."

Judge Belkin responded, "Overruled."

Mr. Trimble coughed and said, "Yeah, it's possible."

"And it's also possible the fire could have been set by someone who had nothing to do with San Jose, correct?" Juan asked.

"Yes," Mr. Trimble responded.

Juan turned to Judge Belkin and said, "I have no further questions for this witness."

Chapter Thirty-seven

April 20, 2009 5:09 p.m.

Judge Belkin dialed James Parker's phone number. It rang a few times until Mr. Parker's voice mail came on.

Judge Belkin said, "This is a message for James Parker. I am Judge Lynda Belkin. We are conducting a hearing. If you receive this message before 5:30, please call (408) 555-4829."

I wanted to throw up my hands and close the case, but I remembered that we still had Brad. I peered at my cell phone and there were still no calls.

I turned to Judge Belkin and said, "Your honor, we may have one more witness. We just need to confer with him."

"Counsel, I already gave you time to confer with your witnesses," Judge Belkin said.

"But your honor, we just need a couple minutes. Not a second more," I pleaded.

"Denied," Judge Belkin replied.

"I don't understand. You gave James Parker twenty minutes to return your call. We still have time."

"Counsel, if you ask me one more time, I will hold you in contempt of court."

Emma made a wry face and said, "Judge Belkin, my life is at stake. For God's sake, we are only asking for a couple of minutes. My life is surely worth that."

Judge Belkin turned to me and scowled, "Counsel, control your client. The court will not tolerate such outbursts."

I fiddled with my cell phone for a second and put it down. "Your honor, we will cease asking the court for additional time. We ask the court to call Brad Culver as our next witness."

Judge Belkin was silent for a few seconds. "Has he agreed to testify?"

"Your honor, as the Chief Assistant District Attorney in Tulare County, Brad Culver is a busy man. Despite his busy schedule, he hasn't told us unequivocally that he will not testify."

"Counsel, answer my question. Did Brad Culver agree to testify?" Judge Belkin asked.

My cell phone began to ring. The caller ID displayed Brad's phone number. "Your honor, Brad Culver is calling us now. I would like to put him on speakerphone."

Judge Belkin glared at me. "You may put him on speakerphone."

I hit the speakerphone button and answered the call. "Dianne Canton speaking."

Brad responded. "Dianne, this is Brad Culver."

"Mr. Culver, we are in Judge Belkin's chambers and we are waiting for your testimony."

Judge Belkin interrupted, "Mr. Culver, this is Judge Belkin. Do you agree to testify?"

There was silence on the other end. Brad then spoke. "No, I do not."

Emma groaned. "Brad, I can't believe you let us down."

Judge Belkin snapped, "Counsel, if your client continues to speak out, you both will be spending a night in jail."

"Your honor, I apologize for petitioner. She will only respond when addressed."

Judge Belkin responded, "It is clear that this witness does not wish to testify. As a result, the court will not be taking his testimony."

"Your honor, petitioner respectfully requests that we treat Mr. Culver as a hostile witness and we have the opportunity to present his testimony," I said.

"Denied," Judge Belkin responded. "That is not within the scope of my ruling."

"But your honor. . ."

"Counsel, stop it now," Judge Belkin ordered. She then turned toward my cell phone and said, "Mr. Culver, you may go now."

Brad responded, "Thank you your honor."

I hit the end button on my cell phone and put it down.

Juan said, "Your honor, because petitioner has no other witnesses, the state asks the court to close testimony."

I interrupted, "It's not 5:30 yet. We still have a few minutes."

"The court will wait until 5:30," Judge Belkin responded. "After that time, all testimony will be closed."

Chapter Thirty-eight

Emma and I sat in silence while we stared at the clock. Second by second passed without a call from James Parker. There were only three more minutes until the judge's 5:30 deadline.

Thirty more seconds passed when we heard a ring from the court's phone. Judge Belkin answered it and put the call on speakerphone.

"This is Judge Belkin. Who is calling?"

"My name is Cynthia Parker. I am James Parker's wife."

"Is Mr. Parker available to testify?" Judge Belkin asked.

"Not right now. He's stuck in traffic and he won't be home for another thirty minutes."

"Mrs. Parker, thank you for informing the court about your husband," Judge Belkin said.

I interrupted, "Mrs. Parker, does your husband have a cell phone?"

"Yes, he does. It's (916) 555-3429," Mrs. Parker responded.

"Thank you Mrs. Parker," I said as I wrote the phone number.

Judge Belkin clasped her hands together. "That will be all Mrs. Parker." She then hung up the phone.

I turned to Judge Belkin and said, "At this time, petitioner respectfully requests that the court call Mr. Parker's cell phone."

Juan interjected, "The state objects."

"On what ground?" Judge Belkin asked.

"It is after 5:30," Juan responded.

"No, it's not. The court's clock says it is 5:29." I countered.

"Your honor, my cell phone says it is 5:31," Juan argued. "This time is accurate, because it is based on a satellite."

"Your honor, the court never stated state counsel's cell phone was designated as the keeper of time," I objected. "The court's clock should be used."

Judge Belkin was silent for a few seconds and then spoke. "The state's objection is overruled. The court will proceed with calling petitioner's last witness James Parker."

I handed the paper with the cell phone number to Judge Belkin. She then dialed the number.

The phone rang a few times until Mr. Parker picked up.

"Mr. Parker, this is Judge Belkin. I am in my chambers with petitioner Emma Watkins, her counsel and the state counsel. Do you willingly agree to testify?"

"Yes, ma'am, but you're difficult to hear. My phone is starting to break-up. Can you call me back in a few minutes when I am at a better spot?" Mr. Parker asked.

"Can you hear me at all?" Judge Belkin asked.

"Yes, but you're not that clear," Mr. Parker responded.

I interjected, "Petitioner respectfully requests an extension of time to call Mr. Parker. The problem with Mr. Parker's cell phone is beyond petitioner's control."

Juan argued, "The state opposes any extension. The court made it clear that 5:30 was the deadline to make the call. The deadline has passed."

Judge Belkin responded, "The court denies petitioner's request for an extension of time. Mr. Parker's testimony will be taken as is."

Judge Belkin quickly administered an oath to Mr. Parker and then turned to me. "Counsel, you may proceed."

"This is Dianne Canton, counsel for Emma Watkins. Mr. Parker did you investigate the fire at the Secretary of State's office in 1987?"

"Yes, I did," Mr. Parker responded.

"Was anyone charged in that case?" I asked.

"The phone is beginning to break-up," Mr. Parker said. "I already sent you an e-mail about what happened."

"Mr. Parker, is your e-mail true and correct?" I asked.

"Yes, it is," Mr. Parker responded.

"Is there anything you want to add?" I asked.

"Yes, there was a possible witness in San Jose," Mr. Parker replied. "He refused to be interviewed."

"Why did you want to interview him?" I asked.

"Because I thought he might be able to give insight on the motive of the two suspects William Eggrose and Barry Bickaree," Mr. Parker responded.

"Do you remember the witness's name?" I asked.

"No, but he was related to one of the suspects."

"Was he one of their friends?"

"I believe he was a cousin of Barry Bickaree," Mr. Parker responded.

"Why did the cousin refuse to testify?" I asked.

"He exercised his fifth amendment," Mr. Parker replied.

"Why do you think he wouldn't testify?" I asked.

"Objection, calls for speculation," Juan roared.

"Objection is denied. Counsel you may proceed," Judge Belkin responded.

"Mr. Parker, again why do you think the witness would not testify?"

"He was this young new lawyer and he didn't want to mess up his bar record," Mr. Parker replied.

"Lawyer? Do you know where he worked?" I asked.

"At the time, he wasn't working," Mr. Parker responded. "He had either resigned or had been fired from his job with the county."

"He worked for the county, correct?" I asked.

"Either the county or the courts, I can't really remember," Mr. Parker replied.

I paused for a couple seconds. "Mr. Parker, was his name Brad Culver?"

"Probably, that name sounds real familiar," Mr. Parker replied.

"Mr. Parker, what do you remember about Mr. Culver?" I asked.

"Ma'am, my phone is breaking up. Can you repeat the question?" Mr. Parker asked.

I repeated the question.

"Ma'am, I'm losing you." The cell phone then went dead.

"Your honor, petitioner respectfully requests that the court grant permission to call Mr. Parker back."

"Denied," Judge Belkin said angrily. "Pursuant to the court's ruling, testimony is now closed."

Juan folded his arms. "Your honor, the state moves that all written declarations including James Parker's shall be deemed to be as inadmissible as evidence on the basis that they are hearsay."

I responded, "Petitioner objects. It is no fault of petitioner that her key witness James Parker's cell phone died. If he had been called back, he would have testified about the money laundering operation not only in Santa Clara County but in other counties as well."

Juan responded, "Petitioner filed her application at the eleventh hour. It was only because of petitioner's procrastination that the witness's testimony could not be heard. The state should not be penalized."

Judge Belkin put her hands on her desk. "All declarations with the exception of the ones provided by the Registrar of Voters and Secretary of State's office will be regarded as inadmissible."

Emma dug her nails into my arm. I removed her hand from me. Judge Belkin glared at us. "Counsel, please control your client."

"Yes, your honor," I replied.

"The court will recess for ten minutes until 5:55," Judge Belkin said. "At that time, petitioner and the state will present their closing arguments."

Chapter Thirty-nine

"Fat-ass bitch," Emma said in the conference room. "And Brad is such a bastard. Give me your cell phone."

I handed Emma my cell phone. Emma dialed Brad's phone number from memory and hit the speakerphone button. After a couple of rings, Brad picked up.

"This is Emma. I want to know the truth now. You were involved with recalling me, weren't you?" Emma asked.

"Emma, what the hell are you talking about?"

"Don't bullshit me. I know that you and Barry Bickaree are related."

"So what, that doesn't mean anything," Brad responded.

"Why wouldn't you talk to the investigator?" Emma asked.

"Emma, that was so long ago. I really don't remember what happened."

"You're full of shit," Emma snapped. "Tell me the truth."

"There's nothing to tell."

"I lost my family, my job and everything. I deserve to know the truth."

"I did, too."

"Bullshit. You were only 27. You moved to Tulare County and became a hotshot in the DA's office."

"It wasn't easy."

"Brad, stop lying to me. You framed me so you could get a prestigious job."

"Emma, you're nuts. My parents practically disowned me when they read about our affair in the paper. Jesus Christ, you were only five years younger than my mother."

"And you knew that when you slept with me. So what's your point?"

"And you were a married woman."

"You weren't innocent. You knew from the beginning everything: our age difference, my marriage and my daughter. I didn't hide anything from you."

"Emma, we never should have been together. It was wrong."

"Don't pretend you didn't enjoy what we had."

"For God's sake, you were sixteen years older than me. It never would have worked."

"It wasn't supposed to. We enjoyed each other's company. And that's all it was."

"Emma, there's no point of rehashing the past."

"My future is on the line, because of the past. And you owe me."

"I don't owe you anything," Brad said.

"I took you in when no one would hire you."

"That's not true," Brad responded.

"Yes, it is. I let you work for me after you repeatedly flunked the bar."

"It took me only four times to pass."

"I passed on my first attempt."

"And look where you are now."

"Go to hell," Emma hissed.

"Emma, I am going to end this call."

"Not until you tell me the truth. You helped the other side recall me."

"That's a lie."

"You gave them my love letters."

"I didn't give them a goddamn thing. They took them from me."

"How?"

"My cousin was visiting me and found them. I didn't know about it until after it came out."

"How the hell did he find them?"

"The letters were in my desk. He was always short on cash. He went looking for money and found the letters instead."

"I thought Barry's father had money."

"Barry could never manage money. He would blow his allowance. After it was gone, Barry's father wouldn't give him a dime more."

"Why didn't you tell me this before?"

"Emma, the past is the past. I can't change it."

"And now you're covering up for your cousin. He caused the fire in Sacramento, didn't he?"

"I don't know what happened."

"Yes, you do. He told you what he did."

"Barry never told me anything."

"Bullshit. I know he told you, because you refused to discuss the case with the police."

"Emma, I need to go now. I have nothing else to say."

"The hell you don't. I lost twenty-three years of my life. I know you know the truth. So just tell me."

Brad took a deep breath and then spoke slowly. "The girl who died was part of the operation of laundering drug money. When she died, they had no choice to do what they did."

"You mean to recall me," Emma said.

"Exactly," Brad said.

"So be a man and tell the truth," Emma said.

"I can't," Brad responded.

"Why not?" Emma asked.

"Because just like you, I have received threats over the years. I can't put my family in jeopardy."

"Brad, we need to go forward."

"I can't. Sorry Emma, I just can't do it."

"You may not have a choice. If I go public with the lottery ticket, everyone will know."

"Emma, for my family, I ask you not to do that."

Emma glanced at her watch. It was 5:54. "Brad, we have to go now. If you see me on the news, you'll know what happened." Emma then hit the end button and handed me the phone.

Chapter Forty

Judge Belkin waved her hand at me and said, "Counsel, you may begin."

I sat in my seat upright and said, "In our nation, we have the constitution. It protects our citizens in order to ensure their rights are not trampled on. As a judge, petitioner followed the constitution in the case of People vs. Rickey Sellers. The defendant's rights had been violated by the San Jose police. They entered Mr. Sellers' apartment without a search warrant and found cocaine and firearms. Their excuse was that the landlord had given them permission. This was clearly a violation of Mr. Sellers' fourth amendment rights. As a judge and a follower of our constitution, my client did the only thing that she could do. She dismissed the case."

"Within a few weeks of Sellers' release, a young woman was allegedly murdered. Mr. Sellers was subsequently charged. Two weeks later, he was found hanging in a jail cell in Elmwood. Next to his body, there was a balled piece of paper scrawled with a confession. The coroner called his death a suicide.

"The San Jose Daily Bullet splashed the confession on the front page and a day later the recall campaign against my client was launched.

"My client's opponents had the perfect case against her. Mr. Sellers was an African-American man who had a history of being in and out of the criminal justice system. The alleged victim was a nineteen-year-old blond, white student at San Jose State. The coup de grace was that petitioner's husband was African-American. So her opponents played the race card, which left my client defenseless.

"It did not matter that my client had followed the constitution. Then there was my client's lapse in judgment. I am not talking about her judicial judgment but her personal judgment. She had an affair with her law clerk who was sixteen years her junior. The media attacked petitioner as if she had committed the worst crime in history. Excerpts from a love letter were published one week before the election. My client lost everything: the election, her stature in the community, and her family.

"But the attacks on my client did not end. Throughout the years, she has received death threats. It was not until a few months ago that they stopped. Petitioner has no idea why they ended.

"There are a lot of unanswered questions in this case. Why did Sellers kill himself? Was he guilty of killing the girl or was he framed? Why were the campaign reports destroyed? Who set the fire? You have heard that the sons of major San Jose political players may have been responsible. Yet, they were never charged. Was this a cover up for the money laundering operation?

"And why did petitioner's former lover Brad Culver refuse to cooperate with the San Jose police in the investigation of the fire?

"And what was Mr. Culver's reason for leaving San Jose? And who helped him get his job with the DA's office in Tulare County? Was it a political payoff or was it based on merit?

"And who gave petitioner's love letters to the media? Was it Brad Culver? Or was it someone else? Again, what was the motive?

"Your honor, there isn't enough time to answer these questions. In less than three hours, the downtown post office in San Jose will close. There are no post offices in Northern California open after 9:00.

"My client must mail in her lottery ticket tonight or she will lose $73 million. If her name is publicized, the threats will begin again and my client may lose her life. My client deserves her right to privacy. The protection of my client's well being clearly overrides the public's interest in the right to know.

"Accordingly, we ask the court to restrain the state from releasing the petitioner's name to the public or the media. Furthermore, we respectfully request that the court accept the deposit of petitioner's lottery ticket. This will ensure that petitioner's interests are protected from any wrongdoing. In closing, we thank the court for its time and consideration."

24 Hour Lottery Ticket

Judge Belkin glanced at her watch and said, "The court will recess for two minutes. When we return, the court will hear the state counsel's closing argument."

Chapter Forty-one

Emma and I walked into the conference room. Emma turned to me and said, "That was a lousy closing argument. A first year law student could have done better."

"I did my best," I responded.

"I'm going to teach you how to be a good lawyer," Emma snapped. "Give me your cell phone."

I handed my cell phone to Emma. She punched in a number and put it on speakerphone. The phone rang a few times until Brad picked up.

"Brad, this is Emma. My lawyer screwed up the case and now we're going public."

"Emma, you can't do that," Brad wailed. "My family can't learn about my past."

"I don't have any options," Emma responded. "I'm not going to lose $73 million over a little publicity. And hell, if they kill me, at least I would have enjoyed life a little bit."

"Emma, you're nuts. No money is worth dying over. And think about me. They could get me, too. And I have a daughter and wife at stake."

"Brad, I've made my mind up. My lawyer has a friend who has media connections and we're calling a press conference in an hour."

"There has to be another way."

"Sorry Brad, you had your chance."

"I didn't think my testimony would have made a real difference."

"Yeah, your testimony could have prevented this from happening."

"I'm sorry. I should have testified. Now, it's too late."

"It's not too late."

"Didn't the judge rule against you?"

"Not yet. My lawyer just did an awful closing and the state's ready to close."

"So what are you saying?" Brad asked.

"Testify now," Emma demanded.

"But Emma," Brad pleaded.

"Don't wimp out on me. If you value your life and family, you'll do it."

"I don't like this."

"In thirty seconds, we're due back in the judge's chambers. Stay on the phone and we'll get you on."

"Shit Emma, you'll piss off the judge."

"So what?"

"And what if she won't let me talk?"

"There are no what ifs. Stay on the goddamn phone and take my lead."

"Will do."

Emma handed me the phone and whispered in my ear. "Don't screw this up."

I nodded as Emma and I got up and walked back into the courtroom.

Chapter Forty-two

I laid my cell phone on the judge's desk and hit the speakerphone button. "Your honor, Brad Culver is now available to testify."

Juan cried out, "Objection, testimony has been closed."

I responded, "Your honor, Mr. Culver's testimony is critical to our case. We will show that the threats against petitioner were not idle, but they were, in fact, very real. The court should allow his testimony."

"Mr. Culver is the Chief Assistant District Attorney. He is not some unschooled witness," Juan objected. "He understands the rules of court. He had his chance."

Judge Belkin clasped her hands. "Objection sustained. Testimony by Mr. Culver is denied."

Brad's voice boomed from my cell phone. "Your honor, I would like to be named as a petitioner in this action."

"On what ground?" asked Judge Belkin.

"For years I received death threats. I have a wife and daughter. If Judge Watkins' lottery ticket winnings are publicized, I am afraid that my family's welfare could be seriously threatened."

"Objection," Juan roared. "If Mr. Culver were truly afraid, he would have testified earlier."

"Counsel is missing a key point," Brad responded. "This is not about simple witness testimony. I have standing to enjoin the Lottery from publishing the results, because my life is at stake. My family and I could suffer irreparable harm."

"Mr. Culver should file his own action," Juan responded.

"Time is of the essence. In less than three hours, Judge Watkins will mail in her ticket. I must be allowed to join now."

"If petitioner mails in the lottery ticket tonight, it may not get to Sacramento for at least a day or two," Juan responded. "Mr. Culver has plenty of time to file his own action."

"Your honor, it will be too late. If the ticket is delivered by overnight mail, it could be delivered as early as tomorrow morning. Once it hits the lottery office, the publicity will happen," Brad responded.

"All of the lottery offices are closed. Our only option is to mail the ticket by overnight mail," I said.

"There's no guarantee that the lottery ticket will arrive tomorrow morning," Juan interjected. "The post office is notorious for delivering mail on an untimely basis. The lottery ticket could arrive in a week, a month or even later."

"State counsel is purely speculating. There could be an earthquake tomorrow or a terrorist attack, but these are not likely to happen," I responded.

Judge Belkin put her hands firmly on her desk. "The court has heard the arguments. It will recess for five minutes. When it reconvenes, a decision about Mr. Culver's motion will be made."

Chapter Forty-three

Emma and I walked into the conference room. I put my cell phone on the table.

"Dammit," Emma howled. "Five minutes is too long to wait."

"Emma, be patient. The judge will rule in our favor," I responded.

"And what if she doesn't?" Emma asked.

Brad said, "And if she doesn't, we'll figure out something else."

"Like what?" Emma asked.

"Maybe there's another way to reach the judge," Brad said.

"What are you saying? Bribery?" Emma asked.

"Of course not," Brad said.

"Then what?" Emma asked.

"There may be others who can influence her," Brad answered.

"Like who?" Emma asked.

"Maybe a husband or significant other," Brad answered.

"Brad, have you lost your mind? Judge Belkin is a big fat woman. She weighs over three hundred pounds. She's not married and there's no way she has a man."

"Not all men are into thin women. Some like big beautiful women. You know women with ample curves."

"Is your wife fat?"

Brad didn't respond.

"I can't believe you're married to a fat woman."

"Elizabeth wasn't always big. After she had Sarah, she couldn't take off the weight. Since then, she's gotten bigger over the years."

"You should dump her."

"It's not about looks. We connect. We have a lot in common and we have a daughter."

"You've changed."

"No I haven't. Just like with you, you were older, but we had a special connection."

"But I was in shape and good looking," Emma scoffed.

"And old enough to be my mother," Brad hissed.

"Go to hell," Emma snapped.

I interjected, "We are really getting off track here. If Judge Belkin rejects Brad's testimony, we need to have a plan."

Brad responded, "I'll figure out something."

"Brad, if you come up with a plan, text-message me."

"Sure," Brad responded.

24 Hour Lottery Ticket

Chapter Forty-four

We reconvened in Judge Belkin's chambers. I gave Judge Belkin Brad's phone number. She dialed his phone number and hit the speakerphone. Brad answered after a couple of rings.

Judge Belkin sat with her hands folded on her desk. "Years ago, when I was a young lawyer, I had a case involving a woman who had been sexually harassed by an older married co-worker. He would tell her how he dreamt about bedding her and how he wanted her. He would cup her breasts and rub himself against her. This was long before Anita Hill and before anyone really knew what sexual harassment was.

"We filed a lawsuit and the company refused to settle. We went to trial. At the end of the trial, another woman came forward. We tried to put her on the stand, but the judge refused to let her testify. We then asked the judge to allow the woman to be another plaintiff in the case. The judge ruled against us."

Judge Belkin paused and unclasped her hands. "I later presented the closing argument. Within an hour, the jury came back. They exonerated the company and the man."

Judge Belkin continued, "The local legal paper ran a blurb about the case and I was devastated. I felt like I was a lousy lawyer and I had no future.

"But after two days, I decided we would appeal. It took two years to reach the California Supreme Court. It later ruled that the trial court was correct in denying the testimony of the other woman.

"However, it also ruled the trial court should have allowed the other woman to join as a plaintiff. They both had similar causes of action against the company and to try them separately would be a waste of the court's resources and taxpayers' money. Consequently, it ordered the trial court to retry the case. When the company heard about the ruling, it offered to settle for $150,000. This may not seem a lot now, but back in the 70s, it was. So we took the settlement.

"We made history with that case and it has been cited in numerous other cases throughout the years. However, I was concerned that the case had been overruled.

"I did a search and the ruling still stands," Judge Belkin said. "The present case involves alleged similar causes of action. Both the petitioner and Mr. Culver have alleged that the publicity will cause them irreparable harm. To try these cases as separate matters would be a waste of the court's resources and taxpayers' money. As a result, the court is hereby allowing Brad Culver to join as a petitioner in the said case."

24 Hour Lottery Ticket

Juan sank in his chair and then straightened his tie. "The state hereby requests the court reconsider its ruling. Your honor, your case involved two women with similar facts. Both had been sexually harassed by the same co-worker. In the present case, the facts are vastly different. Petitioner allegedly possesses the lottery ticket; whereas, Mr. Culver does not. To treat them the same would be a miscarriage of the justice system. It is unfair to the people of California."

"The state's request is hereby denied." Judge Belkin said. "The court shall now swear-in petitioner Brad Culver."

"Your honor, before we begin, I have one request," Brad said.

"What is it?" Judge Belkin asked.

"I would like five minutes to use the bathroom," Brad replied.

"The court will grant you four minutes and not a second more. We will reconvene at 7:07."

Chapter Forty-five

Emma and I walked in silence to the conference room. Once we were inside, Emma patted me on the shoulder. "I can't believe that Judge Belkin came through. For once, she isn't being a bitch."

"Emma, please stop calling her that."

Emma rolled her eyes and said, "She is one most of the time."

I ignored Emma, took my cell phone from my pocket, and put it on speakerphone. I dialed Brad's phone number. Brad answered after the first ring.

"Are you ready to testify?" I asked.

"Absolutely," he said.

Emma grabbed the phone from me and said, "What you say had better be good. If we don't win, our affair will be on the front page of the paper."

"Emma, I'm so tired of your threats. You know you won't go forward if we don't win," Brad responded.

"I will do what it takes to get my money," Emma hissed. "I'm so sick of you, this case and my lawyer who barely passed the bar."

I gave Emma a stern look. "Emma, what are you talking about?"

"Dianne, for Christ's sake, it took you five times to pass," Emma said.

"I'm not ashamed of that," I responded. "A lot of my classmates never passed."

"That's because you went to a law school that doesn't exist anymore," Emma sneered.

"Emma, we really need to focus on the case," I said.

"That's right," Brad said.

"I would expect that from a lawyer who took four times to the pass the bar." Emma said.

"You may have passed the first time and gone to a top law school, but you have nothing," Brad snapped.

Emma opened her mouth and tried to speak. I raised my left hand and made a gesture to Emma to be quiet. "Both of you need to be on your best behavior. That's an order and not a request."

Emma and Brad were both silent. I then ended the call.

I heard a beep from my cell phone. I had a text message. It read: *Baby, I'll do anything to be with you.*

I'm really sorry about Amber and I'm sorry I didn't leave my wife Laura sooner. Love, Shawn.

I stared at the message for a few seconds. I turned around and saw Emma peering over my shoulder.

"Give me your cell phone," Emma demanded.

"Why?" I asked.

"Just do it," she said.

I handed Emma my cell phone. To my dismay, Emma typed a message and sent it. She then handed me back my cell phone.

I pressed the key on my cell phone to show the message. It read: *Shawn, do not contact me anymore. It's over. I need to move on. If you continue to contact me, I will file for a restraining order against you. Dianne.*

"Emma, I can't believe you sent him that," I protested.

"This man is a waste of your time," Emma responded while folding her arms. "Just lose some weight, and then you'll find a man who can give you what you deserve."

I stared at Emma and said nothing. I put my cell phone in my purse.

Emma touched my shoulder and said, "Let's go in now and win this case."

Chapter Forty-six

Judge Belkin dialed Brad's number and hit the speakerphone button. Brad answered on the first ring.

Judge Belkin administered Brad an oath. "Mr. Culver, you may proceed with your testimony."

"Thank you your honor." Brad paused for a couple of seconds and then spoke. "Back in 1984, I was a new law school graduate. I had interviewed for jobs my third year but none felt like a real fit. I saw an ad for a law clerk position in Judge Watkins' court and I applied. The minute I met her I knew there was something about her that was different. She had a special energy that showed she really cared about people. She wasn't some stodgy judge that simply dealt out opinions."

"So counsel, from the beginning you were attracted to her," Judge Belkin interrupted.

"No, not at that time. Judge Watkins was the mentor whom I had been looking for."

"Proceed counsel with your testimony."

"Judge Watkins took me under her wing. She taught me how to appreciate nuances of the law. Deciphering the meaning of case law became a joy. And within a year I was writing opinions for very complex cases."

As Brad spoke, Emma cracked a smile.

"I felt good about my work but things in my personal life were not going well," Brad continued. "I could not pass the bar. I felt like a failure. And after my third attempt, my longtime girlfriend left me. We had been together since my second year in law school. She couldn't deal with my obsession to pass the bar. I felt like my world was coming apart.

"Everyone I knew had passed the bar. I was no longer in their league. I felt like an outcast. So I started coming to work late and calling in sick. My work became sloppy and I didn't care.

"Finally, one day, Judge Watkins asked me what was wrong. I told her everything: my losses and my fears. I expected her to fire me on the spot. Instead, she confided in me. She told me about her loveless marriage and how she wanted to leave but couldn't. A divorced female judge was an anomaly. She felt so alone and she had no one to turn to.

"I don't remember how long it took before we got together. It might have been a couple days or a week. However, once we were, it felt like magic. I felt so alive. When we weren't in the throes of passion, Emma was coaching me on how to pass the bar. It no longer felt like an impossible task. I passed the bar on my fourth attempt."

Brad paused for a few seconds and then spoke. "Emma was assigned to the criminal case calendar. This was a new area of the law and I was so excited. Within a few weeks, the case of Rickey Sellers came before us. Sellers' landlord had given the police permission to search his apartment. His counsel argued for dismissal on the ground that the San Jose police had violated his fourth amendment rights because they failed to obtain a search warrant.

"This was not an easy case. Sellers had been in and out prison. And there was a chance to make new case law in which landlords could become the protectors of the public. Emma and I argued about the case. I felt that we should deny Sellers' motion. Emma felt otherwise. Nothing I said would change her mind. So I wrote the opinion as she wanted it. Sellers was released and within a few weeks, he allegedly killed a San Jose State cheerleader."

"After that, Emma was attacked for her ruling. The recall was later launched. I tried to be supportive in the beginning, but Emma pulled away. And then our affair began to fizzle. I no longer felt connected to her. I wanted to move on.

"Then to my surprise one of the love letters she had written was published on the front page of the paper. God, I felt so ashamed. My parents stopped speaking to me.

"Emma confronted me. I told her I had no idea who had taken the letters to the paper. She called me a liar. A week later, she was recalled and I was out of a job. It wasn't until a month after the election, I found out my cousin Barry Bickaree, who was always broke, had stolen the love letters from my desk. He searched my desk for money and found the letters instead. He then sold them to the recall campaign for a hefty price.

"A few months after the election, I received an anonymous call that the recall committee had been part of a money laundering operation. Over a million dollars in phony contributions and phony expenses had been made. I tried calling Emma, but she refused to talk to me. So I sent her an anonymous letter about it.

"And then there were hang up calls and death threats. I decided to leave San Jose and start all over. I found a job in Tulare County working in the District Attorney's office. Through the years, I've gotten hang up calls and more death threats. The calls finally ended four or five years ago.

"I fear that if Judge Watkins' name is publicized as the lottery winner, the calls and threats will start again. Not only is my life at risk but so are the lives of my wife and teenage daughter. Accordingly, I respectfully ask the court grant my request for a restraining order."

Judge Belkin nodded her head. "Thank you counsel. The court will break for three minutes. We will reconvene for questioning from Emma Watkins' counsel."

Chapter Forty-seven

Emma slammed her purse on the table in the conference room. "Brad is such a liar," she snapped.

"What are you talking about?" I asked.

"He never wrote the opinion in the Rickey Sellers' case. I did."

"I don't think that's relevant. The opinion was based on what you wanted."

"Yes, it was and Brad had nothing to do with it."

"Okay."

"Dianne, you're not getting it. When I heard the case, Brad was in the middle of taking the bar for the fourth time."

"Emma, when did you write the opinion?"

"I took the motion under consideration and followed up with a written opinion a day later."

I pulled out a newspaper article from my briefcase. "It says that you issued the opinion on March 26, 1986. Is that correct?"

"Yes."

"Then Brad wasn't taking the bar. He took it in February."

"You're wrong," Emma argued.

"Emma, I took the bar five times. So I know what I'm talking about."

"You're still wrong," Emma insisted.

"Then google it on my cell phone," I said.

I handed Emma my cell phone. She fiddled with some buttons.

"I'm on the Internet," she said.

"Did you find anything?" I asked.

"I just did a search," Emma replied. "Oh God, you're right. In 1986, the bar was in February. But I still don't remember him writing the opinion."

"Sometimes alcohol impairs the memory," I said.

"Don't insult me," Emma snapped. "The bottom line is that Brad is a liar."

I ignored Emma and looked at my watch. "We need to go back in."

Chapter Forty-eight

"Your honor, I would like to question Mr. Culver," I said.

"You may proceed, counsel," Judge Belkin said.

"Barry Bickaree is your cousin, correct?" I asked.

"Yes," Brad responded.

"Who is his father?" I asked.

"Hayward Bickaree," Brad answered.

"So that would make Hayward Bickaree your uncle, correct?" I asked.

"He was an uncle by marriage," Brad answered. "My aunt and he divorced years ago."

"How long ago?" I asked.

"Back in the early 90s," I said.

"At the time of the recall election, Hayward Bickaree was married to your aunt, correct?"

"Correct," Brad responded.

"What did your uncle do for a living at that time?" I asked.

"He was a real estate developer," Brad responded.

"Wasn't your uncle a major political player in San Jose back in the 80s?" I asked.

"Yes," Brad answered.

"Isn't it true that he contributed to the recall campaign of Judge Watkins?" I asked.

The phone was silent.

"Mr. Culver, I am going to repeat the question. Isn't it true your uncle Hayward Bickaree contributed to the recall campaign of Judge Watkins?"

"I don't know," Brad responded.

"Did anyone tell you that Hayward Bickaree was a contributor to the recall?"

"Objection, calls for hearsay," Brad said.

"Sustained," Judge Belkin responded.

"Isn't it true that you gave your uncle the love letters?"

"Absolutely not."

"Isn't it true you gave your cousin the love letters?"

"Absolutely not," Brad answered. "He stole them from my desk."

"Before the newspaper exposed your affair, isn't it true you told your cousin about it?"

The phone was silent.

"Mr. Culver, please answer my question. Isn't it true you told your cousin about the affair?" I asked.

There was more silence.

Judge Belkin interjected, "Mr. Culver, the court is instructing you to answer the question."

"Yes," Brad responded.

"Isn't it true that you showed your cousin the love letters?"

"Yes," Brad answered.

"When did you show your cousin the letters?" I asked.

"A few weeks before the story broke," Brad responded.

"Why did you show him the letters?" I asked.

"At the time, my cousin was teasing me about the break-up of my ex-girlfriend. It really got to me and I wanted to show him that I had moved on. So I told him about Judge Watkins. When he didn't believe me, I showed him the letters."

"Isn't it true, your uncle paid you for the letters?" I asked.

"Absolutely not," Brad snapped.

"How did you get your job?" I asked.

"I applied for it and I was hired," Brad responded.

"How did you learn about the job?"

"From my law school job placement office," Brad responded.

"Isn't it true that your uncle helped you get the job?" I asked.

"No," Brad responded.

"Are you sure?" I asked.

"Absolutely," Brad snapped.

"I have no further questions," I said.

"The court will recess for two minutes," said Judge Belkin. "When we return, the state shall have the opportunity to cross-examine petitioner Brad Culver."

Chapter Forty-nine

Emma and I walked into the conference room. She pulled my arm and looked up at me into my eyes. "Brad is such a goddamn liar. You should have tried harder."

"Emma, I did everything I could," I responded.

"God, I made a mistake in picking you," Emma said. "You're horrible."

"That's your opinion," I responded.

Emma snapped, "I'm sorry I knocked on your door. It was a mistake."

"If you want me to withdraw from your case, I will," I said.

"It's too late," Emma responded. "I'm stuck with you. We'd better win or else."

I frowned. I then looked at my watch and turned to Emma, "Emma, we need to get going."

Chapter Fifty

April 20, 2009 7:57 p.m.

Judge Belkin motioned to Juan Segura and said, "Counsel, you now may begin your questioning."

"Mr. Culver, you're alleging that you received death threats, correct?"

"Yes."

"What did the caller say?" Juan asked.

"They said that they would kill me and my family if I ever told anyone the truth."

"The truth?" Juan asked.

"About the election," Brad answered.

"What about the election?" Juan asked.

"They didn't say," Brad answered.

"And who were they?"

"I don't know."

"Was it a man or woman?"

"It varied throughout the years."

"You also testified that you received an anonymous call that the recall campaign was part of a money laundering operation, correct?"

"Yes."

"Was the caller a man or woman?"

"A man."

"Do you know who the man was?" Juan asked

"No," Brad answered.

"Did you go to the police about the call?"

"No," Brad responded.

"Why not?"

"Because the caller threatened to kill me."

"You had training as a law clerk handling the criminal calendar, correct?" Juan asked.

"Yes," Brad answered.

"Do you understand police investigation procedures?"

"I do now."

"What about back then?" Juan asked.

"I don't know. I was starting out. I was a novice."

"And yet, you wouldn't go to the police, correct?"

"I told you before that I feared for my life."

"Mr. Culver, you are a seasoned DA, correct?" Juan asked.

"I wasn't back then."

"You stated that you received death threats until four or five years ago, correct?"

"Yes."

"Then why didn't you tell the police about the money laundering operation?" Juan asked.

"I was afraid for my life."

"Is it because there was no money laundering operation and you never received any death threats?"

"No," Brad snapped.

"Mr. Culver, you are testifying under penalty of perjury, please respond with a true answer."

"I am telling the truth," Brad responded.

"Mr. Culver, did you ever apply for a restraining order?" Juan asked.

"No, because I did not know the identities of the parties," Brad answered.

"Yet, every day you prosecute criminals and you couldn't track down the people who were harassing you, correct?"

"Yes, but as you know the law is not black and white. I was not going to use state resources for my case."

"Mr. Culver, in your capacity as an attorney were you ever consulted by a client about the election either before, during or after?"

The phone was silent.

"Mr. Culver, please answer my question." There was no sound from the phone. Juan turned to Judge Belkin and said, "I hereby request that the Court order Mr. Culver to answer my question."

"Your request is granted," Judge Belkin responded.

Brad cleared his throat. "After the election, I had a client who came to me about advice."

"What did he or she want?"

"Your honor, on the behalf of my former client, I am hereby invoking the attorney-client privilege."

Juan interjected, "The crux of this case depends on what Mr. Culver's client told him. Mr. Culver is claiming that he may suffer irreparable harm and yet he refuses to release critical facts that will help determine this. He cannot have it both ways."

Brad responded, "Your honor, with all due respect, the attorney-client privilege can only be waived by the client."

Judge Belkin responded, "The court has heard the arguments and hereby sustains petitioner Culver's request to invoke the attorney-client privilege."

"Mr. Culver, isn't it true the attorney-client privilege can be waived by the client?" Juan asked.

"Yes," Brad answered.

"If your client waives the privilege, you can discuss the case, correct?" Juan asked.

"That is correct," Brad answered.

"What was the name of your client?" Juan asked.

The phone was silent. Judge Belkin tapped her hand on the desk and said, "Mr. Culver, the court is hereby ordering you to answer the question."

"Stephen Eggrose," Brad answered.

Juan turned to Judge Belkin and said, "I hereby ask the court to issue a subpoena for Stephen Eggrose."

"So granted," Judge Belkin responded.

"A subpoena is too late," Brad said. "He died in a car accident a few years ago."

Juan turned to Judge Belkin, "I hereby request that the court reconsider its decision to grant petitioner's motion to invoke the attorney-client privilege. His client is dead. There is no one to protect."

Brad responded, "Your honor, objection. There is ample case law that the attorney-client privilege survives after death."

Judge Belkin responded, "The court denies state counsel's motion to reconsider. The attorney-client privilege cannot be waived."

Juan's face turned red. "Mr. Culver, isn't it true that since your client's death you have not received any threats?"

"I don't remember when the threats exactly stopped," Brad answered.

"Mr. Culver, you said you haven't received threats in the last four or five years. When did Mr. Eggrose die?" Juan asked.

"A few years ago," Brad responded. "I don't remember the exact date."

"A few means three to seven years. How long ago?" Juan asked.

"I don't remember," Brad responded.

"Mr. Culver, does your wife know about your affair with petitioner Watkins?"

"No," Brad responded.

"Does your daughter know about the affair?"

"No," Brad answered.

"Mr. Culver, what does your wife do for a living?" Juan asked.

"She's a doctor," Brad answered.

"How much income does she bring in a year?"

"It varies." Brad responded.

"How much last year?" Juan asked.

"About a half million, " Brad answered.

"How much do you make?"

"$175,000."

"If your wife found about the affair, isn't it true she would leave you?" Juan asked.

"The affair was before my marriage," Brad answered.

"Mr. Culver, I am going to ask you again, isn't it true your wife would leave you if she found out?"

"No," Brad snapped.

"Isn't it true that the real reason you filed this action is you're afraid that if the lottery ticket is publicized you will lose your wife and everything you've worked for?" Juan asked.

"No," Brad answered.

"Come on, Mr. Culver. You and I know better. Eggrose is dead. There haven't been any threats since his death. There's nothing to fear and I remind you again that you are under oath. So I will ask you again, isn't the real reason you filed this action is because you're afraid that your wife will leave you?"

"No, it isn't," Brad answered. "My family's lives are in danger. I cannot in good conscience risk that."

"A dead man cannot threaten you," Juan said. "Stop lying to this court."

"Stop badgering me. I am telling the truth."

Juan turned to Judge Belkin and said, "I have no further questions."

Chapter Fifty-one

Judge Belkin said, "Mr. Culver, please proceed with your closing argument."

The phone beeped a few times.

"Mr. Culver, are you there?" she asked.

"Yes, I'm sorry your honor. Another call came in," Brad responded.

"Please tell the caller to hang up," Judge Belkin said.

"I will." The phone was silent for a few seconds. Brad returned. "I'm sorry again. I'm ready to proceed."

"Go forward," Judge Belkin said.

"Like most people, I've made mistakes with my life. Probably the biggest was my affair with petitioner Emma Watkins. Sleeping with a married woman was wrong and I wish it never had happened. But it did and I cannot change the past.

"The exposure of the affair in the media was not only embarrassing for me, but it was an embarrassment to my parents. It was the worst day of my life. That's why I left San Jose and started all over in Tulare County.

"I excelled at my job in the DA's office. I later met the smartest and kindest woman in the world and she changed my life. Elizabeth introduced me to the church and I became a new person. I learned to enjoy life to the fullest, because I had God in my life.

"I later married Elizabeth. We have a teenage daughter and we are very happy. But there's a dark side that my wife and daughter don't know about it.

"I've never told them about the affair. It happened when I was a very different person. Back then, I was a young man who had failed the bar a number of times. My girlfriend had left me and I felt like nothing. Judge Watkins believed in me and she made me come alive.

"But that does not excuse my affair. It was wrong. Period. I've asked God for forgiveness and if there should come a day in which I need to tell my wife and daughter, I will do it. I know that they will stand by me and my marriage will survive.

"But that is not the reason why I've asked for the restraining order. The real reason behind the recall was the money laundering operation. But unfortunately, I did not have the resources to prove this. Throughout the years, I have received death threats about the recall of petitioner Emma Watkins. The callers told me to never talk about the recall to anyone. If I did, my family and I would lose our lives.

"The threats didn't come from one person. There were men and women who called. I have no idea who they were and I could not trace the calls.

"And yes, it is true they stopped some time after the death of my client Stephen Eggrose. But there is no indication whatsoever that the callers are deceased. So the death threats could start again with the publicity of the lottery ticket."

"And if they do, my family's lives are in danger. I already paid once for the affair. To pay twice with the loss of my wife and daughter is too much to bear. My wife is in the prime of her life and my daughter has her whole life ahead of her. They don't deserve to die for my past mistake. They are innocent and they should be protected at all costs.

"Accordingly, I hereby ask the court to respectfully grant the restraining order and order the Lottery to not release the name of Emma Watkins as the winner of the lottery ticket."

Gayle Tiller

Chapter Fifty-two

April 20, 2009 8:33 p.m.

Judge Belkin turned to Juan and said, "Counsel you may proceed."

Juan began, "Petitioners testified they had an affair over twenty years ago. Petitioner Watkins was a seasoned judge and petitioner Culver was a new law school graduate. She was married and he was single. Some might say there was a disparity in power. Others might say it bordered on sexual harassment. And still others might say the affair was immoral.

"But it doesn't really matter what people think. People are entitled to form their own opinions. That's what America is about -- freedom of speech. Anything short of this would be undemocratic.

"Their affair was later exposed in the media in the midst of the recall campaign of petitioner Watkins. One week later, petitioner Watkins lost the recall

24 Hour Lottery Ticket

election. But despite the recall and media exposure, both petitioners managed to resume their lives. Petitioner Watkins obtained a job at a local nonprofit where she worked until she retired. Petitioner Culver moved to Tulare County where he currently is the Chief Assistant District Attorney.

"Both petitioners allege they received death threats over the years regarding the election. And they alleged the real reason behind the recall was a money laundering operation. Yet, they have no evidence. Former Judge Watkins' own allegation is based on an anonymous letter that she allegedly received from petitioner Brad Culver. And he claims he received an anonymous phone call. The only thing we have left is a hearsay statement from a former investigator. As the court ruled, this statement is not admissible. As a result, the petitioners have no evidence.

"Furthermore, the last death threat petitioner Culver received was several years ago. The death threats stopped for Culver around the time of the death of his client Stephen Eggrose whose son may or may not have been involved with the burning of campaign reports. Of course, this is all speculation. No one was ever charged and no one was ever arrested.

"Emma Watkins' death threats stopped a few months ago. But the key is the death threats stopped for both petitioners.

"Another key is that neither petitioner sought to file restraining orders against the parties who threatened them. I am perplexed why a person like Mr. Culver who works as a Chief Assistant District Attorney would not pursue this remedy. It makes no sense whatsoever.

"Both petitioners say they were unable to track down the culprits. With modern technology, those allegations do not seem credible.

"Petitioners both assume that the media will dig into petitioner Watkins' past and expose the recall election. This is pure speculation. This could or could not happen. And if it does, petitioners have the option of seeking a public relations firm to handle damage control. Celebrities do it all the time.

"And quite frankly, the exposure of an affair is not irreparable harm. Many marriages have survived affairs. And yes, it's possible that petitioner Culver's marriage could break-up and he could lose a lot of income because his wife is a major wage earner. But a break-up of a marriage does not constitute irreparable harm.

"Petitioners also allege the death threats will resume because they both were instructed by the threatening parties not to talk about the recall.

"First of all and most importantly, if the recall is exposed, petitioners are under no obligation to talk about it. Secondly and more importantly, the death threats have not occurred for some time. It is because the threatening parties are most likely dead.

"In petitioner Culver's case, the threats stopped around the time of the demise of his former client. In petitioner Watkins' case, the threats stopped several months ago.

"Because the threats have stopped in both cases some time ago, there is no immediate threat of irreparable harm.

24 Hour Lottery Ticket

"There is a strong public interest in revealing the winner's name. The lottery is operated by the state of California and it provides funding to our state schools.

"To shield the name of the winner of the lottery would be an affront to the good people of California. And the repercussions could be enormous for the lottery program if the court were to set a precedent in granting the restraining orders.

"Californians could lose trust in the program because it would be no longer open and transparent. The program could lose millions of dollars of revenue. This would result in less funding for our schools. Who would get hurt? Our children.

"Do we really want this to happen? No, our children deserve the best quality education and the lottery helps ensure this.

"Accordingly, the state hereby requests the court deny petitioners' request for restraining orders on the basis that it will violate the public's interest and petitioners have failed to demonstrate that they will suffer irreparable harm. And finally, if the court should find in favor of the petitioners, the court shall require petitioner Emma Watkins' lottery ticket is postmarked by 9:00 p.m. by the downtown San Jose post office. If petitioner fails to meet this deadline, her lottery ticket shall have a value of zero dollars."

Juan looked at Judge Belkin directly in the eyes and said, "Your honor, as always, it is a pleasure to appear before you. The state respectfully submits our case and awaits your decision."

Chapter Fifty-three

April 20, 2009 8:41 p.m.

Judge Belkin put her hands firmly on her desk. "The court will first address the petition of Brad Culver for the restraining order. Petitioner Culver has presented an interesting case. For years, he was allegedly threatened by parties unknown regarding the recall of Judge Emma Watkins. At some point, the calls stopped several years ago around the death of a former client who may have been involved with the destruction of campaign reports.

"Petitioner Culver has argued that if petitioner Watkins' name is released, he and his family will suffer irreparable harm. His reasoning is that the death threats may occur again.

"The court has reviewed the facts and cannot in good conscience grant petitioner Culver's request. Firstly and most importantly, the court finds that the death threats are unlikely to occur again.

"Secondly, the release of the name of Emma Watkins may create a media frenzy in which his past affair is revealed. While this may have an impact on petitioner Culver's marriage and family, this does not constitute irreparable harm.

"Thirdly, the issuance of a restraining order would set a bad precedent. If members of the public are given the unfettered right to restrain the release of lottery winners' names, it would open Pandora's box. The public could lose faith in the lottery, because its operations no longer would be open and transparent.

"Sales could plummet and less revenue would be generated for our schools. This could create a dire situation for our schoolchildren.

"Accordingly, the court hereby denies petitioner Culver's request for a restraining order."

Emma's face turned a bright red as she dug her hand into my thigh and whispered, "Do something."

I wrote on my pad: *I can't. You need to be quiet.*

Emma whispered back, "If you don't do something now, I will destroy you.

I wrote: *Don't threaten me.*

Emma rolled her eyes and said nothing.

Judge Belkin glared at us. "Counsel, the court will not tolerate inappropriate facial expressions by your client."

"Your honor, they were unintentional. Petitioner has the upmost respect for this court."

"Thank you, counsel," Judge Belkin responded. "The court will recess for five minutes and will reconvene at 8:54 p.m. for its decision on the petition of Emma Watkins."

I nodded my head and beckoned Emma to follow me.

Chapter Fifty-four

April 20, 2009 8:49 p.m.

I turned to Emma and said, "There's no way we'll win this case. We need to turn in the ticket. The post office is a seven-minute walk. If we leave now, we'll make it before the 9:00 deadline."

Emma gave me an angry look and said, "Dianne, we're not giving up."

"Emma, you need to be realistic. The judge ruled against Brad. She'll do the same thing with us."

Emma folded her arms. "Brad deserved to lose. His testimony and argument were horrible."

"But Emma, I don't see how we will prevail."

"We will win."

"If we lose, there's no way we can make it in time to the post office. You'll lose everything."

"Screw the goddamn post office. We will fight until the end."

"I think you're making a really bad decision," I said.

"Dianne, my decision is final," Emma responded.

I stared at Emma for a few seconds and said nothing. I then looked at my watch.

"Emma, if I call Robyn, she'll be able to get some great publicity. We can hold a press conference tomorrow morning."

Emma's eyes narrowed. "A press conference is unacceptable."

"She'll be able to put a great spin on your story," I argued.

"I won't do it," Emma snapped.

"Emma, we need to call Robyn now. She's our only hope."

Emma's face turned a bright red and she shook her fists in the air. "You will not call her. Period."

I pulled my cell phone from my purse.

"Dianne, put your goddamn cell phone away," Emma yelled.

"I won't let you lose $73 million," I responded.

"If you call her, I will make sure that you never practice law again."

I stared at Emma for a few seconds. I then slowly put my cell phone inside my purse. "Emma, you win."

"Good," Emma said. "Let's go back in."

I nodded my head and followed Emma into the courtroom.

Chapter Fifty-five

"Now, the court shall rule on the petition of Emma Watkins," Judge Belkin said. "Petitioner was a judge who was recalled about twenty-three years ago. At that time, her extramarital affair was revealed in the newspaper and other media.

"As recently as a few months ago, Petitioner received death threats from unknown parties. Prior to filing this case, petitioner never filed a restraining order. Her argument is that she could not file because she did not know the identities of the parties. Furthermore, petitioner never contacted the San Jose Police Department for assistance.

"Petitioner's phone number is public and she has the option of making it private. However, she does not want to do this, because she hopes that her estranged daughter will contact her for reconciliation.

"Petitioner is afraid that if her name is released, the threats will not only continue but they will escalate

24 Hour Lottery Ticket

to unbearable levels. The threats may come to fruition, which could result in her death.

"There also is a strong public interest in this case. The lottery must be open and transparent. If it is not, our schoolchildren will ultimately lose.

"This is a very difficult case for the court. Some may argue that petitioner put herself in this situation by her extramarital affair years ago. She was married and sixteen years older than her law clerk. She should have known better and her actions may have been immoral or bordered on sexual harassment.

"However, this court does not adjudicate on the issue of morality. Only God or a higher power, if one exists, can do this.

"Nor has petitioner been charged with sexual harassment. The issue before this court is whether the Lottery Authority should be restrained from releasing her name.

"After examining the facts of this case, the court hereby finds that petitioner will suffer irreparable harm with the release of her name. This clearly outweighs the public's interest. As a result, her petition for a restraining order is granted.

"Secondly, given the fact that the downtown post office closes in approximately four minutes, it is highly unlikely that petitioner will be able to obtain a postmark by 9 p.m. By failing to meet the 9 p.m. deadline, petitioner's ticket will become worthless, because there are no other post offices open in Northern California after this time.

"To grant a restraining order for an invalid lottery ticket is no remedy at all. Accordingly, the court orders petitioner to deposit her lottery ticket by 9 p.m. with this court. The acceptance of the lottery ticket by this court shall constitute compliance of meeting the Lottery Authority's deadline.

"Furthermore, the court issues the following additional orders: 1) The Lottery Authority will independently verify that petitioner is the winner within a timely matter; 2) In any statement to the media, the Lottery Authority will state it is restrained from releasing the name of the winner; 3) This case is sealed; and 4) In all references to this matter, petitioners shall be referred herein as Jane Doe and John Doe."

Emma smiled and pulled from her purse the lottery ticket and handed it to Judge Belkin.

"The court has received and accepted the said lottery ticket at 8:57 p.m. This court is now adjourned."

Emma and I got up and walked out of the judge's chambers. Emma gave me a hug and said, "I knew we could do it. You're great lawyer."

"Thank you, Emma," I responded. I put my hand into my pocket, took out the charm, and gave it to Emma.

"You can keep it." Emma smiled.

"No, it's yours. Please take it back," I responded.

"It was your father's," Emma said. "He gave it to me a couple days before he died. He wanted you to have it."

"Thank you," I replied. "I'm glad the charm worked."

"Indeed, it did," Emma said while nodding her head.

"What was my father like?" I asked.

"Sometime over dinner I will tell you," Emma responded.

"I'm starving," I said. "Let's go to dinner now."

"I'd like to celebrate, but I have somewhere else I need to go."

"Oh," I said with disappointment.

"I have a date," she responded. "If you go out, order from the low calorie menu. And stay away from dessert, because you can't afford to gain another pound."

"Will do," I sighed.

"Thanks again for everything."

"You're welcome."

Emma and I walked out of the courthouse and departed our separate ways.

Chapter Fifty-six

Emma walked into my office. Several weeks had passed since I had last seen her. The media had run numerous stories about Judge Belkin's decision. Many had attacked it and a few had applauded it.

Emma sat down and crossed her legs, "Dianne, I still owe you $500 plus the contingency fee of $125,000." She reached into her purse and pulled out a check.

"Dianne, pay off your bills and find a decent apartment," Emma said while handing me the check. "An office is no place for a woman to live."

I nodded my head and said, "Thank you."

"I hope you're staying away from Shawn," Emma said.

"I am," I answered.

"Good," Emma smiled. "Just lose some weight and you'll find someone decent."

"Sure," I responded.

"Thanks for everything. You were worth it," Emma said as she got up from her chair.

I made a gesture for her to stay. "Emma, I know the case is over but I have one question that has been bothering me. I can't figure out why the death threats stopped earlier for Brad."

"Brad lied about the threats," Emma answered.

"Why?" I asked.

"To protect his wife," Emma responded.

"From learning about your affair?" I asked.

"Don't be silly," Emma said. "She always knew about it."

I looked at Emma in disbelief. "He lied."

Emma nodded her head. "After the case I hired a private investigator who found out that Brad and his wife Elizabeth met shortly after the recall," Emma responded. "At the time, her father was the police chief in San Jose. One night during a drunken binge, Elizabeth told Brad that her father had taken over $100,000 in bribes from a drug cartel. He needed the money to pay off his gambling debts.

"The drug cartel was controlled by the Eggrose family. They had laundered millions of dollars of drug money through various political campaigns throughout

California. The committee that had recalled me was part of this covert operation.

"Brad was deeply in love with Elizabeth and did not know what to do. He couldn't go to the police, because Elizabeth's father was involved. But he still had an allegiance to me. So Brad sent me an anonymous letter.

"Somehow Elizabeth learned about the letter. She then told her father about it. Her father told Stephen Eggrose who later had the copies destroyed in the fire in Sacramento. Because the originals of the reports were housed in various counties, they couldn't destroy them. So they defaced the reports with white correction fluid. Somewhere around that time that's when the death threats against me began.

"To make sure that Brad would be prevented from talking about anything, Stephen Eggrose contacted Brad for legal advice. In exchange, he arranged through his political connections that Brad start as a deputy district attorney in Tulare County.

"Brad had no prospects in San Jose. So he took the offer. Elizabeth and he got married and the rest is history."

Emma paused for a few seconds. She then spoke. "With no publicity, Elizabeth's secret is safe forever. And the past will remain in the past."

"So we made a mistake in contacting him," I said.

"Maybe," Emma responded, "But now he knows that I know the truth."

"How?" I asked.

"After the investigation, I called Brad and told him about my private investigator's findings."

"And he confirmed everything?" I asked.

"Of course not," Emma answered. "He's not stupid."

"Aren't you afraid that the death threats will start up again?"

"No, I'm not," Emma answered. "Now he knows that I know the truth, the threats will never happen again."

"Emma, isn't that blackmail?" I asked.

"No, it's insurance," Emma answered. "I can lead a full life and my past is no longer a burden."

"That's good," I said. "Speaking of the past, when are we going to dinner to talk about my father?"

"Dianne, not today," Emma responded. "But someday we will."

Emma shook my hand and walked out of my office. I watched her from my door as she got into her battered Mustang. She smiled as she waved goodbye.

Epilogue

January 20, 2010

Since our meeting, I hear from Emma from time to time. She's still chasing younger men and hasn't given up her drinking. But life's a little better with the lottery winnings. Emma moved out of senior housing and bought a small house downtown.

Emma and I still haven't met for dinner to talk about my father. But I'm hoping that we will meet soon.

With the contingency fee from the case, I've paid off my bills, moved into a cheap apartment and bought a second-hand car. I haven't gotten any major cases yet but at least I'm still in business. Considering we're in a recession, that's an accomplishment.

I haven't talked to Shawn since the case ended. And I finally bought a scale. I was shocked when I saw the number. It got me motivated to start an exercise program. I haven't lost any weight yet. Maybe it's because I'm still eating a few scoops of rocky road ice cream every day.

24 Hour Lottery Ticket

Until I find someone who is truly single, I'm going to stick to rocky road ice cream for pleasure. If that's my only vice, I think I'm doing pretty well. It beats dating married men.

Made in the USA
Charleston, SC
15 June 2010